The Kiss of the Spider Woman

Book by **Terrence McNally**
(Based on the novel by **Manuel Puig**)

Music by **John Kander**
Lyrics by **Fred Ebb**
Directed by **Harold Prince**

IMPORTANT BILLING AND CREDIT REQUIREMENTS

All producers of KISS OF THE SPIDER WOMAN must give credit to the Author and Composer of the Play in all programs distributed in connection with performances of the Play and in all instances in which the title of the Play appears for purposed of advertising, publicizing or otherwise exploiting the Play and/or a production. The names of the Author and Composer must also appear on a separate line, on which no other name appears, immediately following the title, and must appear in a size of type not less than fifty percent of size of the title type. Billing must be substantially as follows:

(NAME OF PRODUCER)

PRESENTS

"KISS OF THE SPIDER WOMAN-THE MUSICAL"

Book by	Music by	Lyrics by
Terrence McNally	John Kander	Fred Ebb

Based on the novel by
Manuel Puig

Originally directed by
Harold Prince

KISS OF THE SPIDER WOMAN - THE MUSICAL

opened June 14, 1992 at the Bluma Apple Theatre - St. Lawrence Centre for the Arts in Toronto, Canada with the following cast:

Molina	BRENT CARVER
Warden	HERNDON LACKEY
Valentin	ANTHONY CRIVELLO
Esteban	PHILIP HERNANDEZ
Marcos	MICHAEL McCORMICK
Spider Woman/Aurora	CHITA RIVERA
Aurora's Men	KEITH McDANIEL, ROBERT MONTANO, DAN O'GRADY, RAYMOND RODRIGUEZ
Molina's Mother	MERLE LOUISE
Marta	KIRSTI CARNAHAN
Religious Fanatic/Prisoner	JOHN NORMAN THOMAS
Amnesty International Observer/Prisoner	JOSHUA FINKEL
Prisoner Fuentes	GARY SCHWARTZ
Gabriel/Prisoner	JERRY CHRISTAKOS
Window Dresser at Montoya's/Prisoner	AURELIO PADRON

STANDBYS & UNDERSTUDIES

Standbys and understudies never substitute for listed players unless a specific announcement for the appearance is made at the time of the performance.
Standbys—for Spider Woman/Aurora: DOROTHY STANLEY
for Molina's Mother: LORRAINE FOREMAN; for Marta: SUSAN GILMOUR.
Understudies—for Molina; Joshua Finkel; for Valentin: Philip Hernandez, Gary Schwartz; for Esteban: Gary Schwartz; for Marcos: John Norman Thomas; for Warden: Michael McCormick; for Gabriel: Dan O'Grady; for Amnesty International Observer: Gary Schwartz.
Swing—KELLY PATTERSON.

STAGE MANAGEMENT

ProductionStage Manager: STEPHEN CROUCH; Senior Stage Manager: SUSAN KONYNENBURG; Stage Managers: OLWYN LEWIS, KIM SMITH

KISS OF THE SPIDER WOMAN ORCHESTRA

Conductor: JEFFREY HUARD
Violin/Viola: ARTUR JANSONS (Concert Master), CLAUDIO VENA;
Viola: SYLVIA LANGE, JONATHAN CRAIG; Principal Cello: GISELA DEPKAT;
Bass/Electric Bass: DAVE YOUNG; Woodwinds: MARK PROMANE, VERNE DORGE, HARVEY KOGEN, BOB LEONARD; Principal Trumpet/Flugelhorn: ARNE CHYCOSKI;
Trumpet/Flugelhorn: SANDY BARTER; Principal French Horn: GARY PATTISON;
French Horn: TERESA WASIAK; Trombone: AL KAY; Drums: KEVIN McKENZIE;
Percussion: MARTY MORELL; Keyboard: KERRY McSHANE, MICHAEL MULROONEY
Assistant Conductor: MICHAEL MULROONEY
Orchestra Contractor: MOE KOFFMAN

KISS OF THE SPIDER WOMAN - THE MUSICAL
opened October 20, 1992 at the Shaftesbury Theatre
in London with the following cast:

Molina ....BRENT CARVER
Warden... HERNDON LACKEY
Valentin ....ANTHONY CRIVELLO
Esteban.. PHILIP HERNANDEZ
Marcos... MICHAEL McCORMICK
Spider Woman/Aurora.. CHITA RIVERA
Aurora's Men ....KEITH McDANIEL, ROBERT MONTANO,
DAN O'GRADY, RAYMOND RODRIGUEZ
Molina's Mother.. MERLE LOUISE
Marta.. KIRSTI CARNAHAN
Religious Fanatic/Prisoner ....JOHN NORMAN THOMAS
Amnesty International Observer/Prisoner...............JOSHUA FINKEL
Prisoner Fuentes ....GARY SCHWARTZ
Gabriel/Prisoner ....JERRY CHRISTAKOS
Window Dresser at Montoya's/Prisoner ....AURELIO PADRON

STANDBYS AND SWINGS
Standbys—Spider Woman/Aurora and Marta DOROTHY STANLEY
Molina's Mother LORRAINE FOREMAN
Swings—CADET BASTINE, COLTON GREEN

STAGE MANAGEMENT
Company Stage Manager: NICK EARLE; Production Stage Manager: PAT THOMAS
Stage Managers: CAMILLA CLUTTERBUCK, SIMON DODSON
Assistant Stage Managers: TERRY ELDRIDGE, PATRICIA SWALES

THE KISS OF THE SPIDER WOMAN ORCHESTRA
Musical Supervisor/Conductor: JEFFREY HUARD
Musical Director: GARETH VALENTINE
Concert Master (Violin/Viola): MARTIN TURNLAND;
Violin/Viola: DAVID LYON; Liola: LYNNE BAKER, KAREN DEMMEL;
Cello: DAVID BUCKNALL; Bass: DAVE OLNEY;
Woodwinds: JOHN WHELAN, PETE LONG, ALAN SHEPPARD, JAY CRAIG;
Principal Trumpet/Flugelhorn: JIM WILSON;
Trumpet/Flugelhorn: DUNCAN SMITH;
Principal French Horn: HUW EVANS; French Horn: JANE HANNA;
Trombone: ADRIAN LANE; Drums: GRAHAM WARD;
Percussion: PETER FARMER; Keyboard: GEOFF EALES, PETER McCARTHY

Assistant Musical Director: PETER McCARTHY
Orchestra Contractor: MAURICE CAMBRIDGE
for Accord Music Productions Ltd.

KISS OF THE SPIDER WOMAN - THE MUSICAL,

opened Monday, May 3, 1993 at The Broadhurst Theatre,
New York City with the following cast:
(in order of appearance)

Molina	BRENT CARVER
Warden	HERNDON LACKEY
Valentin	ANTHONY CRIVELLO
Esteban	PHILIP HERNANDEZ
Marcos	MICHAEL McCORMICK
Spider Woman/Aurora.	CHITA RIVERA
Aurora's Men/Prisoners	KEITH McDANIEL, ROBERT MONTANO, DAN O'GRADY, RAYMOND RODRIGUEZ
Molina's Mother	MERLE LOUISE
Marta	KIRSTI CARNAHAN
Escaping Prisoner.	COLTON GREEN
Religious Fanatic/Prisoner	JOHN NORMAN THOMAS
Amnesty International Observer/Prisoner Emilio	JOSHUA FINKEL
Prisoner Fuentes	GARY SCHWARTZ
Gabriel/Prisoner	JERRY CHRISTAKOS
Window Dresser at Montoya's/Prisoner	AURELIO PADRON

STANDBYS & UNDERSTUDIES

Standbys & Understudies never substitute for listed players unless a specific
announcement for the appearance is made at the time of the performance.
Standbys: for Spider Woman/Aurora and Marta—DOROTHY STANLEY;
for Molina's Mother—LORRAINE FOREMAN

Understudies: for Molina—Joshua Finkel; for Valentin—Philip Hernandez, Gary
Schwartz; for Esteban—Gary Schwartz; for Marcos—John Norman Thomas; for
Warden—Michael McCormick; for Gabriel—Dan O'Grady; for Amnesty International Observer—Gary Schwartz.

Swing—GREGORY MITCHELL
Partial Swing—COLTON GREEN

Conductor—Jeffrey Huard

Assistant Conductor—Greg Dlugos
Concert Mistress—Susan Follari
Musical Coordinator—John Monaco

1st Trumpet—Jeffrey Kievit; 2nd Trumpet—Larry Lunetta; Trombone—Porter Poindexter;
French Horns—Kate Dennis, Susan Panny; Reed I—Al Hunt; Reed II— Mort Silver; Reed
III—Richard Heckman; Reed IV— Ken Berger; Bass—John Babich; Drums—John
Redsecker; Percussion—Mark Sherman; Keyboard I— Jeff Saver; Keyboard II—Greg
Dlugos; Viola I—Susan Follari; Viola II—Ann Barak; Viola III—Matine Roach; Viola
IV—Katherine Sinsabaugh; Cello—Caryl Paisner..

SCENES AND MUSICAL NUMBERS

The action takes place in a prison in Latin America,
sometime in the recent past.

ACT I

ENTR'ACTE

ACT II

OVERTURE

(Music cue #1)

SPIDER WOMAN: *(A voice in the darkness as the curtain opens, revealing MOLINA seated on his cot.)*

COME AND FIND ME
HEAR MY SONG
LET ME HOLD YOU HERE WHERE YOU BELONG

(Lights come up on PRISONERS upstage walking in an exercise circle.)

LIPS ARE WAITING
PAIN WILL CEASE
CALM YOUR ANGUISH I CAN BRING YOU PEACE

(A momentary BLACKOUT on everyone but MOLINA. The lights then come up to reveal the PRISONERS behind bars in the prison.)

PRISONERS:
AH - UH!
AH - UH!
AH - UH!

AH - UH!
AH - UH!
AH!

(A man - VALENTIN - is dragged onstage by two guards - MARCOS and ESTEBAN.)

ACT I

Scene 1

(TWO GUARDS are leading a young man - VALENTIN. The WAR-DEN appears on the catwalk. The PRISONER and his TWO GUARDS freeze in a spotlight.)

WARDEN. Prisoner 16115. Name - Valentin Arrequi Paz. Age 27. Arrested July 7th at Las Vantas Metro stop. Apprehended in act of passing travel documents to political fugitives. Suspect is key link to terrorist groups. Prisoner has been brought to La Hermosa State prison where he is now being held under executive power of the Federal government and awaiting judgment. *(VALENTIN and the two GUARDS start off.)* Prisoner is currently being interrogated. We will break him. I assure you he will be broken. We have ways. (We hear a blood-curdling scream offstage.)
   SPIDER WOMAN (V.O.):
SOONER OR LATER
YOU'RE CERTAIN TO MEET
IN THE BEDROOM, THE PARLOR OR EVEN THE STREET

(The YOUNG MAN we have previously seen--VALENTIN--is dragged, unconscious, across the stage floor and thrown brutally into MOLINA'S cell. He lands face down so that his face is not visible to MOLINA. The GUARDS start to exit.)

ESTEBAN. *(Leaving.)* Hey Molina, you little queer. Here's a new leading man for one of your movies.
   MARCOS. He's just your type.

(They exit. MOLINA remains cowering by his cot. He does not look at the unconscious figure with him. The WARDEN reappears on the catwalk. He shines the searchlight brightly on MOLINA.)

WARDEN. Prisoner 57884. Name--Luis Alberto Molina. Age 37.
Sexual offender. Arrested for corrupting a minor. Male. Serving third
year of eight year sentence.

*(He switches searchlight off and exits. **Music cue #2 "AURORA"
under:**)*

MOLINA. Aurora, help me! What movie? There were so many.
What scene? Aurora, I need you. Come to me, like you always have.
HER NAME IS AURORA
AND SHE IS SO BEAUTIFUL
NO MAN WHO HAS MET HER CAN EVER FORGET HER
THEY'RE MADLY IN LOVE
FOREVER IN LOVE
    I see her so clearly. I know her so well.

*(Upstage, a white scrim in the shape of a movie screen through which
    we see AURORA in a bathtub attended by servants. They are all
    male - a BUTLER, a VALET, a CHAUFFEUR, a MASSEUR, for
    example. AURORA rises from the tub as MOLINA sings:)*

SHE STEPS TO HER GLASS NOW
ALL ALMONDS AND ROSES
SHE'S POWDERED AND PAMPERED
THE SIGHT OF HER DARK EYES
IGNITING THE SCREEN...
SCORCHING THE SCREEN.

(Lights out on cell. We are totally in the 'movie'.)

SERVANTS:
LOOK AT HER RADIANCE
SEE HOW SHE GLOWS
LOOK AT HER SILKEN CHEEKS
PINK AS A ROSE
TELL US YOUR SECRET MA'AM
TELL US PLEASE DO
WHAT IS THIS HAPPINESS
SHINING FROM YOU?

AURORA:
SO, YOU WANT TO KNOW
WHY I'M AGLOW
OH!

LAST NIGHT, I WENT TO SEE THE GYPSY
AND OH, THE THINGS SHE HAD TO SAY
SHE TOLD ME I WOULD MEET A STRANGER
A LEAN, HANDSOME HERO
WHO'D SWEEP IN AND SWEEP ME AWAY

I SAT THERE TREMBLING AT HER TABLE
AND SMELLED THE INCENSE IN THE AIR
"SOMEDAY, YOU'LL HEAR A CRY", SHE TOLD ME
"A SHARP, PIERCING SOUND
AND WHEN YOU LOOK AROUND
THE LOVE OF YOUR LIFE
WILL BE THERE!"

(AURORA dances with her MALE SERVANTS.)

COMPANY:
OOH!
OOH!
OOH!
AURORA:
"I CANNOT TELL YOU HOW YOU'LL MEET HIM
OR WHEN YOU'LL MEET YOUR LOVE OR WHERE
BUT SOON, YOU'LL HEAR THAT CRY", SHE TOLD ME
"AND YOU'LL LOOK AROUND,"
SERVANTS:
YOU'LL LOOK AROUND!
AURORA:
"AT THAT SHARP, PIERCING
ALL:
SHARP PIERCING
SHARP PIERCING
SHARP PIERCING
SHARP PIERCING

(The cell lights up and we see VALENTIN turn over and let out an agonizing scream. The number comes to an abrupt end as MOLINA rushes to VALENTIN'S body and kneels over him.)

MOLINA. Oh, my God. I didn't know how they'd hurt you. I didn't look. *(To VALENTIN.)* You'll be alright. Take deep breaths, it helps. I'll tell you about my Aurora. I'll tell you her movies, her wonderful movies! We'll be friends. I need a friend. My name is Molina. You can trust me.

(Suddenly, a light beams down on MOLINA. Standing on the catwalk is the WARDEN.)

WARDEN. I do, Molina. I trust you completely.

(BLACKOUT)

Scene 2

(Music cue # 3 "OVER THE WALL 1")
(Lights up on the prison cells. The various PRISONERS are leaning through the bars in various postures. The first PRISONER starts to sing.)

FIRST PRISONER:
THERE ARE BIG BUSTED WOMEN
OVER THE WALL
   ALL:
OVER THE WALL
   FIRST PRISONER:
THERE ARE BIG BUSTED WOMEN
WHO BAKE ON THE BEACHES
WITH OIL ON THEIR BELLIES
OVER THE WALL
   ALL:
OVER THE WALL
   SECOND PRISONER:
THERE IS RUM FROM THE CANE FIELD
OVER THE WALL
   ALL:
OVER THE WALL

SECOND PRISONER:
THERE IS RUM FROM THE CANE FIELD
IN ROUND BULGING BARRELS
IT BURNS WHEN YOU SWALLOW
OVER THE WALL
   ALL:
OVER THE WALL
   3RD PRISONER:
THERE IS SUN ON MY TAXI
   4TH PRISONER:
AND CAKES IN MY OVEN
   5TH PRISONER:
AND FISH IN MY NETTING
   6TH PRISONER:
AND GEESE IN MY BARNYARD
   ALL:
AND BIG BUSTED WOMEN
OVER THE WALL
OVER THE WALL
OVER THE WALL
   SECOND PRISONER:
AND I WONDER *IF* I'LL EVER SEE THEM AGAIN

*(The lights start to fade. THE SPIDER WOMAN suddenly appears
  on the catwalk.)*
(Music cue #3A "SPIDER WOMAN" FRAGMENT 1.)

   SPIDER WOMAN:
AND THE MOON GROWS DIMMER
AT THE TIDE'S LOW EBB
AND YOUR BREATH COMES FASTER
AND YOU'RE ACHING TO MOVE.
BUT YOU'RE CAUGHT IN THE WEB...

        (BLACKOUT)

*(Immediate lights up on the cell. MOLINA is on his cot and VALENTIN
  sits reading on his.)*

Scene 3

(Music cue #4 "BLUEBLOODS")
(The cell. MOLINA unrolls a movie poster of AURORA in "Forbidden Love". VALENTIN pays no attention.)

MOLINA:
DO YOU KNOW WHY THEY CALL ROYALTY BLUEBLOODS?
WELL, I DO.
THEY CALL ROYALTY BLUEBLOODS BECAUSE THEIR SKIN
        WAS SO THIN
THAT THEIR VEINS SHOWED THROUGH.
BLUE!
THERE! THAT'S SOMETHING I'VE TAUGHT YOU.
(Pause.)
NO NEED TO THANK ME.
    VALENTIN. Go to hell!
    MOLINA:
ANY MORE THAN YOU EVER THANKED ME
FOR NURSING YOU THROUGH THOSE FIRST FEW DAYS
WHEN THEY FIRST THREW YOU IN HERE
REMEMBER THAT?
VALENTIN, MEET MOLINA, THE RESIDENT QUEEN
WELL, I SUPPOSE SOME PEOPLE ARE ALWAYS THE
        UNGRATEFUL KIND
LIKE YOU. TO NAME A FEW.
YOU! YOU! YOU! YOU! YOU!
    VALENTIN:
WILL YOU PLEASE SHUT UP
WILL YOU EVER SHUT UP?
CAN'T YOU LEAVE ME ALONE?
THERE'S A SIDE OF THIS CELL THAT'S YOUR OWN.
WITH IT'S OWN SPACE, IT'S OWN AIR
STAY THERE?

(MOLINA makes a motion to button his lip. There is silence for some time. Then MOLINA, unable to stand it, finally speaks.)

    MOLINA. We're going to be together for some time. You'd think you'd want to know something about me. *(Silence.)* I did re-do the cell in your honor! I should have done it sooner but they transferred me so many times, to so many cells, usually solitary. I was beginning not to care. So, you see, this splendor is al for you. Of course, dressing things up is my specialty. I'm a window dresser at Montoya's, their main store, thank you very much, the one right on Plaza Mayor. I'm good at it, too. And do you know why? Thanks for asking. It's because I can't rest until each mannequin is perfect.

(Music cue #5 "DRESSING THEM UP/I DRAW THE LINE")

DRESSING THEM UP
I LOVE THE DRESSING THEM UP
THE SUBTLE TILT OF A HAT
TOUCHES LIKE THAT
MAKE ME
THE BEST OF THE LOT AT
DRESSING THEM UP

I WAS THE CREAM OF THE CROP
THE WAY I BUCKLED THE BELT
FOLDED THE FELT
HELPED ME TO GET WHERE I GOT
BEFORE I GOT WHERE I GOT
I WAS THE ABSOLUTE TOP

FOR EXAMPLE...

ONCE, I ASKED FOR A BALENCIAGA SCARF
TO STUFF IN A MANNEQUIN'S PURSE
THEY TOLD ME, "NO ONE ON EARTH WILL SEE"
I ANSWERED "NO ONE ON EARTH BUT ME"
AND I STOOD MY GROUND AS NO OTHER DRESSER DOES
AND DARLING GUESS WHAT?
BALENCIAGA IT WAS!

DRESSING THEM UP
I WAS THE CREME DE LA CREME
AS I ADJUSTED EACH HEM
I KEPT ON DAZZ-A-LING THEM
AT MY PARTICULAR STORE

WHICH WAS THE BEST IN THE TOWN
YOU'D NEVER CATCH THEM WEARING A FROWN
OR CATCH THEM DRESSING ME DOWN
FOR MY FINESSE AT
DRESSING THEM UP.

RAISE THAT SKIRT
JUST AN INCH OR TWO
ADD SOME ROUGE
JUST A PINCH OR TWO
START THE FAN
NO, MUCH GUSTIER
STUFF THAT GAUZE
MAKE HER BUSTIER
OOH, THAT FROCK
TOO MUCH RED IN IT
I WOULD NOT
BE CAUGHT DEAD IN IT
WELL, THEY START OUT LIKE HELL
BUT I MAKE THEM SELL BY
DRESSING THEM UP
FROM EARRINGS DOWN TO THEIR BOOTS
IN EVENING DRESSES OR SUITS
UNLIKE SOME SECOND RATE FRUITS
AT OTHER SECOND RATE STORES
WHICH CAN'T COMPARE TO MY OWN
YOU'LL NEVER CATCH THEM WEARING A FROWN
OR CATCH THEM DRESSING ME DOWN
FOR MY FINESSE
AT DRESSING THEM UP!

I HAD THE TOUCH
THANK YOU VERY MUCH!
        VALENTIN:
WILL YOU PLEASE SHUT UP
WILL YOU EVER SHUT UP?
(MOLINA pantomimes buttoning his lip. VALENTIN mimicking:)
"THANK YOU VERY MUCH."

YOU'RE MAKING ME SICK
WITH THAT PRISSY WHINE
WATCH ME NOW. I DRAW A LINE.

SO YOU STICK TO YOUR SIDE
AND I'LL STICK TO MINE
NEVER, EVER CROSS THIS LINE
    MOLINA:
FINE!
BUT THE POT
HOW ABOUT THE POT?
    VALENTIN:
WHAT ABOUT THE POT?
    MOLINA:
IT'S ON YOUR SIDE
    VALENTIN:
SO WHAT?
    MOLINA:
SO WHEN I HAVE TO USE THE POT
I INTEND TO USE THE POT
    VALENTIN:
SO WHAT. THAT'S AN EXCEPTION.
    MOLINA:
OH, GRACIOUS ONE. THANKS A LOT.
    VALENTIN:
SO DON'T EVER TRY TO BE
DON'T EVER DREAM YOU'LL BE
DON'T DARE TO THINK THAT YOU'LL
EVER BE SOME FAIRY
FRIEND OF MINE
CAUSE NO NO NO NO
THAT'S WHERE I DRAW THE LINE.
    MOLINA. Fine!
    VALENTIN:
I DRAW THE LINE
    MOLINA. Fine!
    VALENTIN:
I DRAW THE LINE

(At the song's finish, MOLINA, strutting about, still can't seem to get VALENTIN'S attention away from the book he is reading. MOLINA peers over the 'line' and speaks.)

MOLINA. What are you reading? The complete works of Karl Marx? Oh, that sounds like fun. *(In an exaggerated basso.)* "The struggle is not over until all men are free". I know! Dolores Del Rio said that in "RECKLESS IN RIO". *(In falsetto.)* "The struggle is not over until all men are free".

(MOLINA pantomimes being shot by a firing squad.)

VALENTIN. *(To MOLINA on the floor.)* Even ridiculous faggot window dressers who won't shut up!
MOLINA. *(Getting up.)* Stick to the script, please. Marx didn't say 'ridiculous'.
VALENTIN. Marx didn't spend three days in a cell with you.
MOLINA. Five days. You weren't conscious the first two. For that matter, I'm not sure you're conscious yet. *(VALENTIN sits up on his cot.)* Oh, I better watch my step. I heard how you Marxists like to take advantage of a girl who's down on her luck. *(He begins to yell and bang the cell bars. PRISONERS join in offstage.)* Guards! Guards! He's trying to convert me. He's putting ideas into my dizzy head. He's making me forget the simple joys of fascism.

(MOLINA'S yells have attracted the attention of MARCOS and ESTEBAN. They come rushing to the cell door.)

MARCOS. QUIET! *(To MOLINA.)* What do you want, Molina?
MOLINA. Nothing, I was just fooling around.
ESTEBAN. I know what someone like Molina wants.
MOLINA. You're not man enough to give it to me.

(MOLINA is immediately sorry he said this.)

ESTEBAN. What?
MOLINA. Nothing.
ESTEBAN. What did you say, you miserable little...
MOLINA. Nothing. I said nothing.
MARCOS. You said something Molina.

(The TWO GUARDS have drawn blackjacks.)

MOLINA. I said I'm a piece of shit.
MARCOS. Louder.
MOLINA. I said I'm a piece of shit.
MARCOS. Louder.
MOLINA. I said I'm a piece of shit.
MARCOS. I still can't hear you.
MOLINA. I said... please don't make me.
MARCOS. Ah, ah, ah! Finish it, maricon, you're almost done.
MOLINA. I said I'm a faggot piece of shit and anytime you want me, I'm here.
MARCOS. Maybe later, sweetheart.
ESTEBAN. *(Prodding VALENTIN on his bed.)* Hear that, 16115? Anytime you want her, she's all yours. Ain't you the lucky one? Oh, maricon, why are you crying? For your sins? For breaking your mama's heart?

(The GUARDS exit. MOLINA is on his knees, embarrassed and ashamed. VALENTIN raises himself on an elbow and looks at MOLINA.)

VALENTIN. Why do you let them humiliate you like that?
MOLINA. I don't let them. I'm a coward. *(Pause.)* Besides darling, there are privileges in degradation. It got me my ravishing drapes and my pin-ups.
VALENTIN. *(Dismissing him.)* Make yourself trivial.
MOLINA. We're both trivial. The only difference between us is that I know it and you don't.
VALENTIN. You go to hell.
MOLINA. We're already there.
VALENTIN. I will go mad alone in this cell with this person!
MOLINA. *(Compassionately.)* Do you have a girl? Try thinking of her. It helps. I've got a girl.
(Music cue #6 "DEAR ONE)

VALENTIN *(To himself):*	**MOLINA:**
MARTA, WHERE ARE YOU?	Does that surprise you?
MARTA, I NEED YOU	I think of her nearly
MARTA, DON'T LEAVE ME NOW	all the time.
DON'T LET ME GO CRAZY	

MOLINA. *(Rattling on.)* My mother. How do you thank a person who's given you her life? Not like this. I only pray she's forgotten all about me.

(MOLINA'S MOTHER appears. The WARDEN appears.)

    WARDEN. Not a chance, maricon, not a chance.
    MOTHER:
DEAR ONE
NO, I DON'T THINK ABOUT YOU
DEAR ONE
I DO NICELY WITHOUT YOU
DEAR ONE--SAY THAT OVER AND OVER
KEEP REPEATING IT AS THE DAYS GO BY

(MARTA appears in the cell.)

MARTA:	**MOTHER:**
DEAR ONE	
NOTHING WARM IS DENIED ME	DEAR ONE
DEAR ONE	
I DON'T MISS YOU INSIDE ME	DEAR ONE

    MARTA AND MOTHER:
DEAR ONE
SAY THAT OVER AND OVER
KEEP REPEATING IT AS THE DAYS GO BY
AND SOMEDAY YOU'LL BELIEVE THE LIE

VALENTIN:	**MARTA:**	**MOTHER:**
DEAR ONE		
I AM THROUGH WITH		
CRUSADING	DEAR ONE	
	ALL MY ANGER	
	IS FADING	DEAR ONE

    VALENTIN AND MARTA:
DEAR ONE
SAY THAT OVER AND OVER
KEEP REPEATING IT'
AS THE HOURS FLY

MOLINA:
DEAR ONE

I DON'T SEE YOU CROCHETING

MOLINA: **MARTA:**
DEAR ONE NOTHING WARM IS
DENIED ME
I CAN'T HEAR
WHAT YOU'RE
SAYING I DON'T MISS YOU
INSIDE ME

MOTHER AND VALENTIN:
DEAR ONE

MOLINA AND MOTHER:
SAY THAT OVER AND OVER
KEEP REPEATING IT

KEEP REPEATING IT
AS THE HOURS FLY
AS THE DAYS GO BY

VALENTIN:
AND SOMEDAY

MOTHER:
SOMEDAY

MOLINA:
MAYBE

MARTA:
MAYBE
YOU'LL BELIEVE

MOTHER, MOLINA, VALENTIN:
YOU'LL BELIEVE

ALL:
THE LIE

MOTHER:
NO I DON'T THINK
ABOUT YOU
I DO NICELY
WITHOUT YOU

VALENTIN:
DEAR ONE

DEAR ONE

VALENTIN & MARTA:
DEAR ONE
SAY THAT OVER
AND OVER
KEEP REPEATING IT
AS THE HOURS FLY

(Music continues under as MOTHER and MARTA fade away.)

(BLACKOUT)

Scene 4

(Muisc cue #7 "OVER THE WALL 2")
*(Lights up on PRISONERS. A large fence is now stretched across the
    downstage area.)*

THREE PRISONERS:
WHERE IS THE WOMAN I CALL MY WIFE?
WAITING FOR ME TO RESUME MY LIFE?
GUARDING HER ASS WITH A KITCHEN KNIFE?
OR SCREWING THE JANITOR
OVER THE WALL.

WHERE IS THE FRIEND IN THE PHOTOGRAPH
TENDER AMIGO WHO MADE ME LAUGH
SPLITTING THE SHIT WITH ME, HALF AND HALF
IS HE TAKING GOOD CARE OF IT
OR STEALING MY SHARE OF IT?
OVER THE WALL

(Lights up on MOLINA.)

MOLINA:
SO I SIT ON MY COT AND MY MEMORY WHIRLS
AS I THINK OF THE BOYS DRESSING UP LIKE GIRLS
WEARING TOO MUCH MASCARA AND PHONY PEARLS
OVER THE WALL.

(MARCOS and ESTEBAN enter.)

MARCOS. Hey, Molina, the Warden wants to see you.

(As VALENTIN watches, MOLINA exits with the GUARDS.)

PRISONERS:
WHERE ARE THE CHILDREN WHO BEAR MY NAME?
MAKING A CIRCLE TO PLAY A GAME?
DO THEY SAY TO THE NEIGHBORS I'M NOT TO BLAME?

OR SPIT AT THE THOUGHT OF ME
OVER THE WALL.

(Suddenly the lights come up on the WARDEN.)

WARDEN. Do not think for a moment that those of us who guard these animals are not compassionate men. We encourage hope here, dreams. When they lose their precious sleep and spend the night digging pathetic little holes in the walls of their cells, did we not supply them with the spoons and the cups they dig with? And, in the morning, when they cover their handiwork with posters and clothing, we pretend not to see. As I've said, we encourage hope here. See him? (He points to man crawling behind the DS fence.) See that animal? We've let him believe he can escape, that's all. We are... after all... compassionate men.
   VALENTIN:
SO, I WAIT IN MY CELL FEELING HALF ALIVE
SHARING FOOD WITH A RAT, MAYBE FOUR OR FIVE
WHILE THE RATS WITH THE POWER CAN ALL SURVIVE
OVER THE WALL

(The PRISONER now lunges desperately to the fence. He starts to climb it frantically.)

   VALENTIN AND PRISONERS:
OVER THE WALL
OVER THE WALL
OVER THE WALL
OVER THE WALL
OVER THE WALL
OVER THE WALL
OVER THE WALL
OVER THE WALL
OVER THE WALL
OVER THE WALL

(A siren sounds and when the PRISONER is almost at the top a GUARD--ESTEBAN--pinpoints him with his searchlight.)

(At the same moment, another searchlight pins him from the front. We hear the sound of rapid machine gun fire. The PRISONER hangs dead on the fence. We light up again on the PRISONERS in their cells. SPIDER WOMAN appears.)

VALENTIN AND PRISONERS:
OVER THE WALL
OVER THE WALL
OVER THE WALL

(BLACKOUT)

Scene 5

(Music cue #7A "PRISON UNDERSCORE 1")
(MOLINA and VALENTIN are discovered. VALENTIN shows some signs of the beating he's taken. MOLINA, as usual, is chatting away.)

MOLINA. What makes you think we were bourgeois? Because I love movies? Darling, I was a *cineaste* in my mother's womb. *(Beat.)* That shut you up!

VALENTIN. *(Angry.)* All right, what's a *cineaste?*

MOLINA. A movie addict, stupid.

VALENTIN. Don't call me stupid.

MOLINA. Don't call me bourgeois. We didn't have a pot to piss in. After my father died, my mother had to work nights as an usher-ette in a cinema. She never complained. I, of course, adored it. It was a fabulous cinema. It had Egyptian decor. Since there was no one to look after me, she took me with her and sat me in the front row. I was this big. Everyone on the screen was enormous. That's where I first saw my Aurora. My mouth dropped open. It still is open. *(From off-stage we hear a terrifying scream. VALENTIN turns to listen. MOLINA keeps rattling on.)* She was everything.

VALENTIN. Ssshh.

MOLINA. Don't ssshh me. I'm talking about Aurora. I saw every movie she ever made over and over and over. And I loved them all. They're all right here--*(He points to his temples.)* Every line, every song, every costume, every kiss. I loved them all--even the ones she made in Hollywood! *(We hear another scream sounds from offstage. MOLINA blithely continues.)* All except one. She scared me. It was about a woman who was death. They called her the Spider Woman. When she kisses someone--a child even--they died. I couldn't look. I began to cry. Mama said it was only a movie, only a part she was playing, but Mama was wrong. She's real, the Spider Woman is. She's here. I know it. I've seen her.

(We hear another scream.)

VALENTIN. Shut up, you fool. Listen.

MOLINA. I don't hear what I don't want to hear.

VALENTIN. More foolishness. You and your Aurora.

MOLINA. Oh? What about you and your Marta?

VALENTIN. Where did you hear that name?

MOLINA. You talk in your sleep.

VALENTIN. What did I say?

MOLINA. Nothing. Just Marta. It was the way you said it! You're crazy about her, aren't you?

VALENTIN. I thought you didn't hear what you don't want to hear.

MOLINA. Oh, but I did want to hear about that, especially when you were saying what it was you'd like to do to her.

VALENTIN. Shut up! Just shut up! Besides, what do you care? I thought you like boys.

MOLINA. I do, but I'm always willing to broaden my horizons. *(Staring at him provocatively. After a pause.)* Don't worry darling. You're not my type. I'm looking for someone to settle down with, not storm the barricades.

VALENTIN. When you're not molesting minors in some men's room.

MOLINA. I didn't know he was a minor! When he smiled at me, I thought he was smiling at someone else. Men like me don't get smiled at a lot. But he kept smiling. So I smiled back. I followed him right into a trap. And it wasn't a men's room. It was a coffee bar. *(We hear another scream.)* They're bringing a prisoner and they're going to make us look at him to frighten us. I'll look but I won't see. Deaf, dumb and blind. Take my advice, Mr. Revolutionary.

(*Music cue #8 "WHERE YOU ARE"*)
  MOLINA:
WHEN YOU FEEL YOU'VE GONE TO HELL IN A HANDBASKET
AND THE WORLD IN WHICH YOU DWELL'S NO PARADISE

(The side curtain opens to reveal AURORA as she continues the song
    while MOLINA mouths the words:)
  AURORA:
I'VE SOME COUNSEL I CAN GIVE
YOU NEED BUT ASK IT
I'M SO VERY GLAD TO SHARE THIS GOOD ADVICE

YOU'VE GOT TO LEARN HOW NOT TO BE
WHERE YOU ARE
THE MORE YOU FACE REALITY, THE MORE YOU SCAR
SO CLOSE YOUR EYES AND YOU CAN BE A MOVIE STAR
WHY MUST YOU STAY WHERE YOU ARE?

YOU'VE GOT TO LEARN HOW NOT TO SEE
WHAT YOU'VE SEEN.
THE SLICE OF HELL YOU CALL YOUR LIFE IS HARSH AND
        MEAN
SO WHY NOT LIE BESIDE ME ON A MOVIE SCREEN
WHY MUST YOU SEE WHAT YOU'VE SEEN?

(ESTEBAN and MARCOS enter with prisoners in chains.)
  AURORA:
AND IF YOU FIND THAT YOU LAND IN JAIL
A LITTLE FANTASY WILL NOT FAIL
IT'S JUST AS SIMPLE AS ABC
COME UP HERE. PLAY WITH ME. PLAY WITH ME.

YOU'VE GOT TO LEARN HOW NOT TO DO
WHAT YOU'VE DONE
THE PISTOL SHOT CAN'T KILL IF YOU UNLOAD THE GUN.
SO BUILD A PALACE WHERE YOU'RE THE SHAH
AND WE'LL EMBRACE IN THAT SHANGRILA.
IF YOU RUN AWAY, SOME MATINEE
FROM WHERE YOU ARE.

(BRIDGE - pauses (2x8). Prisoners enter behind panels.)

AURORA AND PRISONERS: *(In a whisper.)*
YOU'VE GOT TO LEARN HOW NOT TO BE
WHERE YOU ARE
THE MORE YOU FACE REALITY THE MORE YOU SCAR
SO CLOSE YOUR EYES AND YOU'LL BECOME A MOVIE STAR
WHY MUST YOU STAY WHERE YOU ARE?
(Percussion chorus (4x8) AURORA continues:)
AURORA:
SO WHY NOT LIE BESIDE ME ON A MOVIE SCREEN
WHY MUST YOU SEE WHAT YOU'VE SEEN?
AURORA AND PRISONERS:
AND IF YOU FIND THAT YOU LAND IN JAIL
A LITTLE FANTASY WILL NOT FAIL
IT'S JUST AS SIMPLE AS ABC
AURORA;
COME UP HERE. PLAY WITH ME.
PRISONERS:
PLAY WITH ME.
YOU'VE GOT TO LEARN HOW NOT TO DO
WHAT YOU'VE DONE
THE PISTOL SHOT CAN'T KILL IF YOU UNLOAD THE GUN.
AURORA:
SO BUILD A PALACE WHERE YOU'RE THE SHAH
AND WE'LL EMBRACE IN THAT SHANGRILA.
IF YOU RUN AWAY, SOME MATINEE
FROM WHERE YOU ARE.

(BRIDGE (2x8) DANCE BREAK (12x8)
AURORA:
AND IF YOU FINE THAT YOU LAND IN JAIL
A LITTLE FANTASY WILL NOT FAIL
IT'S JUST AS SIMPLE AS ABC
COME UP HERE. PLAY WITH ME.
PRISONERS:
COME UP HERE. PLAY WITH ME.
AURORA:
TURN OFF THE LIGHTS AND TURN ON YOUR MIND
AND I CAN PROMISE YOU YOU WILL FIND
YOU WILL LIKE MY PLAN, MY SWEETEST FAN,
MY LEADING MAN
ANYWHERE YOU ARE.

(AURORA and MALE DANCERS freeze in place as ESTEBAN and MARCOS drag on a PRISONER with a cloth sack over his head.)

ESTEBAN. Recognize this one, Valentin? *(They pull a bag off the PRISONER'S head. VALENTIN recoils at the sight.)* A friend of yours?
    VALENTIN. I've never seen him before.
    MARCOS. You sure? Look again.

(MUSIC as AURORA and the PRISONERS shift their stance. The WARDEN appears on the catwalk.)

WARDEN. Get him out of here. When he comes to, question him again. Not so nice this time.

(They drag the PRISONER off. VALENTIN has begun to tremble uncontrollably at the thought of what is going to happen to him.)

MOLINA. I've seen that one around the yard. I think his name is... What's the matter? I *told* you not to look! *(MUSIC cue #8A PRISON UNDERSCORE 2 as AURORA and the PRISONERS shift their stance.)* Did you recognize him?
    VALENTIN. I wouldn't tell you if I did.
    MOLINA. Darling, if I looked like her, I'd wear a bag over my head too.
    VALENTIN. *(Grabs him roughly.)* Shut up! You and your stupid movies and you Aurora and you shawls. You disgust me.
    MOLINA. It was a lousy joke. I'm sorry.
    VALENTIN. I'm not one of your goddamn movies. I will probably die here, and I will have accomplished nothing *but* my death. Nothing. Don't insult my life even more. Look at me. I'm shaking. I'm as pathetic as you.

(BLACKOUT)

Scene 6

(WARDEN appears with and OBSERVER from Amnesty International. OBSERVER looks like a businessman in his suit and tie.)

WARDEN. I thought you were observing *prison* conditions here and all the time what you really wanted to talk about were human rights. First, let's define "human"--then we'll talk about "rights".

OBSERVER. Amnesty International doesn't believe you can separate the two.

WARDEN. Amnesty International isn't running a hopelessly overcrowded prison.

OBSERVER. You have a political prisoner here, one Valentin Arregui Paz.

WARDEN. Never heard of him.

OBSERVER. We have reports he's been tortured unmercifully.

WARDEN. I don't know what you're talking about.

(As WARDEN and OBSERVER move off, lights up on a cell, packed exactly as the OBSERVER described it. MOLINA and VALENTIN are among the undulating mass of bodies.)

PRISONER #1. Mary, Mother of God, help me!

PRISONER #2. Shut up with that stuff. She ain't going to get us out of here.

PRISONER #3. Three days they've kept us on our feet!

PRISONER #4. Stop counting!

PRISONER #5. I can't breathe, I can't breathe.

PRISONER #6. You know why they're doing this, don't you? Him. That new guy. Valentin. He's the reason.

PRISONER #7. Give them what they want, goddamit!

MOLINA. He's on your side, Fuentes.

PRISONER #7. Nobody's on my side in this hellhole but me, Molina.

MOLINA. Shut up, Fuentes. All right, whose hand is that?

PRISONER #6. Mine. I'm sorry, Molina.

MOLINA. Leave it there. I love it.

PRISONER #9. What time is it.

PRISONER #4. *(A terrifying attack of claustrophobia.)* I'm not going to make it.

MOLINA. Think about your wife and children, Raymondo.

VALENTIN. *(Low, to MOLINA.)* Molina! This one, he's dead.

MOLINA. *(Low, to VALENTIN.)* You just noticed? Sshh! *(Loud.)* Okay, everyone! We will now sing our National Anthem: *(He sings.)* "Deutschland, Deutschland Uberalis"

(No one joins in.)

PRISONER #7. Talk, goddamnit, Valentin, Talk.
MOLINA. He doesn't know anything.
(Music cue #9 "OVER THE WALL 3" - MARTA)
VALENTIN: *(Starting front)*
THERE'S A COBBLESTONE STREET
AND A LITTLE RED DOOR
AND THREE FLIGHTS UP IS MARTA
WAITING THERE IS MARTA
PRISONERS:
OVER THE WALL
OVER THE WALL

VALENTIN:
AND I STILL CAN SEE US LYING TOGETHER
TALKING, SMOKING, LYING TOGETHER
AND THE THOUGHT OF BEING TOGETHER
HELPS ME THROUGH

SO I CLOSE MY EYES
AND I HEAR HER STEP
AND I KNOW SHE'S COME TO HOLD ME
SO MY SENSES STIR
PRISONERS:
OVER THE WALL

VALENTIN;
BUT IT'S NEVER EVER HER
IT'S JUST A DREAM OF HER
PRISONERS:
OVER THE WALL
OVER THE WALL
OVER THE WALL

VALENTIN:
SO, I CLOSE MY EYES
AND I HEAR HER STEP
AND I KNOW SHE'S COME TO HOLD ME
SO, MY SENSES STIR

PRISONERS:
OVER THE WALL
OVER THE WALL

VALENTIN:
BUT IT'S NEVER EVER HER
IT'S JUST A DREAM OF HER
PRISONERS:
AND I WONDER
IF I'LL EVER SEE THEM AGAIN

(BLACKOUT)

Scene 7

(Music cue #10 "INTERROGATION")
(Lights up on WARDEN and MOLINA.)

WARDEN. Sit! Molina, we believe this Valentin has a girlfriend who's the key to everything. We catch her, their pathetic little group is finished. Perhaps he's told you about her? No? He hasn't mentioned a name?

MOLINA. Fascist! Pig! Fascist pig! Murdering fascist pig bastard! You mean like that, warden?

WARDEN. I mean this girlfriend's name!

MOLINA. No. Nothing.

WARDEN. We have ways, Molina. Need I remind you? *(Lights up on ESTEBAN and MARCOS. They are making ready to torture him, as described by the WARDEN.)* A metal bucket over a man's head--that bucket struck with batons. *(To PRISONER.)* Last chance, amigo.

(ESTEBAN and MARCOS raise their batons to strike. Lights down.)

(The orchestra simulates blows to the bucket as an introduction to the SPIDER WOMAN who is discovered looking down on the scene.)

*She is suspended above in a giant spider web which she navigates
predatorily.)*

SPIDER WOMAN:
COME - I AM THE ANSWER
COME - I CAN STOP THE PAIN
COME - I AM THE RAINBOW THAT FOLLOWS THE RAIN

COME AND GIVE ME
YOUR CARESS
HEAR MY CALL AND ANSWER YES, YES.

(Lights up on WARDEN and MOLINA.)

WARDEN. Welcome back, Molina. Still nothing for me? He hasn't
mentioned her yet, not even in his sleep?

MOLINA. Maybe he did. How would I know, warden? I was
sleeping too.

WARDEN. Then I suggest you sleep less and listen more. We
have another kind of persuasion. Falaca! Sounds like a dance step.
Amnesty International calls it cruel and inhumane torture than can
cripple a man for life. Get me this whore's name, Molina...!

*(The GUARDS make ready to beat the soles of the PRISONER'S feet.
Lights down as SPIDER WOMAN sings.)*

SPIDER WOMAN:
COME - I'M THE SOLUTION
COME - EVERLASTING REST
COME - PLACE YOUR HEAD ON MY WELCOMING BREAST

(Lights up on the PRISONER and GUARDS.)

ESTEBAN. He's dead.

*(Music up as the PRISONER gets up from the chair and slowly starts
climbing the web to reach the SPIDER WOMAN.)*

(Lights up on MOLINA and WARDEN.)

WARDEN. Ah, Molina, my friend! I'm afraid I have bad news for you. Your mother, she's very sick.

MOLINA. When? What happened? How do you know?

WARDEN. Find out for yourself, Molina. Life awaits you outside these walls. Life and your mother. His girlfriend's name is your key to freedom. No? Bring in the next one!

(ESTEBAN and MARCOS exit.)

(Lights up on SPIDER WOMAN. As she sings, the DEAD PRISONER begins climbing the bars to reach her at the center of her web.)

SPIDER WOMAN:
COME - I AM THE ANSWER
COME - I CAN STOP THE PAIN
COME - I AM THE RAINBOW THAT FOLLOWS THE RAIN
COME AND FIND ME
HEAR MY SONG
LET ME HOLD YOU
HERE WHERE YOU BELONG
COME! COME!

(ESTEBAN and MARCOS return. Open cell door--revealing VALENTIN. The SPIDER WOMAN kisses the DEAD PRISONER, who drops from the bars.)

(BLACKOUT)

Scene 8

(Lights up on a row of cells. ESTEBAN and MARCOS enter with a man who has a hood over his head. ESTEBAN and MARCOS drag VALENTIN between them stopping at each cell. In a cell PRIS-ONER is singing.)

PRISONER:
JESUS THOU ART COMING
HOLY AS THOU ART
THOU THE GOD WHO MADE ME
AND MY SINFUL HEART

(In another cell a PRISONER is standing on his head.)

MARCOS. Hey, Fuentes. You want to see something pretty?
FUENTES. You call that pretty? That's not pretty. I'll show you
something pretty. *(He moons the GUARDS.)* Go to hell.
ANOTHER PRISONER. Yeah, go to hell!
ESTEBAN. Who said that? Who said that?
FUENTES. My asshole said it.
MARCOS. Come on Esteban. They're animals.

(ESTEBAN and MARCOS move on.)

PRISONER:
JESUS THOU ART COMING
HOLY AS THOU ART
THOU THE GOD WHO MADE ME
AND MY SINFUL HEART

MARCOS. Jesus can't help you stupido!
ANOTHER PRISONER. Shut up will ya?!
PRISONER:
JESUS THOU ART COMING
HOLY AS THOU ART

*(In the next cell a man sits huddled on the floor clenching his knees
to him. He rocks back and forth and mumbles.)*

ESTEBAN. How you doing, clown?

*(ESTEBAN and MARCOS move on. A man is pacing back and forth
endlessly.)*

MARCOS. Hey, Emilio! You'll make a hole in the floor walking back and forth like that.

EMILIO. A hole, yes. Then I'll escape through that hole. I'll run from you bastards.

ESTEBAN. But first see what you'll look like when we catch you.

(ESTEBAN removes the hood from the man's head. He lifts the man's slumped over face and holds it up by his hair.)

EMILIO. You think you frighten me? Huh? (*Frightened but defiant, he walks to the man and through the bars takes his face in his hands. Then rubs the blood all over EMILIO'S face.*) I can't be frightened. See!

(ESTEBAN and MARCOS move on. A man is standing, clutching the bars and staring straight ahead.)

CARLOS. What time is it? Please. They never tell you what time it is in here.

MARCOS. Hey, amigo. Recognize Molina's little boyfriend?

PRISONER. Father, forgive them, for they know not what they do.

(BLACKOUT)

MOLINA: *(In the dark as the cell moves downstage.)*
HER NAME IS AURORA...
AND SHE IS SO BEAUTIFUL...
NO MAN WHO HAS EVER...

(The Lights come up on MOLINA and the cell.)

CAN FORGET, FORGET, FORGET!

(The MUSIC stops. MOLINA looks at VALENTIN lying unconscious on his cot, bloody and beaten.)

MOLINA. Oh, God. Sweet Jesus. How much can you endure? And

I'm sure you still didn't give them the names they want. Why don't you?

(MOLINA goes behind the curtain to get a cloth for VALENTIN'S wounds. Light change reveals the silhouettes of two figures behind the curtain. MOLINA and AURORA.)

AURORA. How is he? I want to see him.
MOLINA. Aurora, I don't know how much more he can endure. What makes a man like that so brave?
AURORA. Love, you fool, love!
(Music cue # 11 "I DO MIRACLES")
AURORA:
I DO MIRACLES
THOUGH THE LASH OF THE WHIP HAS CAUSED YOUR
        FLESH TO TEAR
I WILL PLACE MY LIPS ON YOU EVERYWHERE
AND I'LL DO MIRACLES.

BLOOD
ON YOUR SLENDER HIPS
BLOOD
UNDERNEATH YOUR EYES

BLOOD
ON YOUR FIRM YOUNG THIGHS
LET ME KISS IT AWAY
SO THAT I CAN HEAR YOU SAY
THAT
I DO MIRACLES

THOUGH YOUR BREATH RACKS YOUR RIBS AND YOU
        THROB WITH PAIN
THERE'S A JUICE ON MY LIPS FOR EACH PURPLE STAIN
AND MY HAIR SWEEPS YOUR CHEST LIKE A COOL,
        BLACK RAIN
YOU CAN'T EXPLAIN
BUT YOU WILL SEE
I DO MIRACLES
THERE ARE MIRACLES IN ME.

(We hear MARTA'S voice as VALENTIN imagines it and perhaps we see her face isolated in space.)

MARTA:
I DO MIRACLES
   AURORA:
I DO MIRACLES
   MARTA:
AS I CRADLE YOU CLOSE AND CARESS EACH BRUISE
WHAT I'VE COME HERE TO GIVE, YOU MUST NOT REFUSE
   BOTH:
THERE IS LOVE IN MY TOUCH THAT IS YOURS TO USE
AND IF YOU CHOOSE
JUST BREATHE MY NAME
AND THERE I'LL BE
DOING MIRACLES
I DO MIRACLES
THERE ARE MIRACLES IN ME

(BLACKOUT)

Scene 9

(Darkness.)

VOICE. *(On tape.)* Raymondo, Hernandez. Fuentes. *(Lights come up on MOLINA setting a makeshift table in the cell. He places a colorful napkin at both settings. MARCOS and ESTEBAN are handing plates through the cell door to VALENTIN.)* Molina, Paz. Rodriguez, Carlos.

VALENTIN. *(Touching napkins.)* Where did these come from?

MOLINA. My mother. She came to visit the last time you were in interrogation. I told you that.

VALENTIN. Interrogation. I knew there was a word for it. Thank you. I was calling it torture.

MOLINA. Owww! Is that a glimmer of a sense of humor? And I left my sun glasses in   the corniche.

VALENTIN. I thought your mother was sick.

MOLINA. She was sick, but now she's well enough to visit. You don't (didn't) listen.

VALENTIN. Are you an informer, Molina?

MOLINA. What do you take me for? I'm angry you'd even think (you should even suggest) such a thing.

(Music cue 11A "WARDEN UNDERSCORE')

WARDEN. *(Appearing on the catwalk.)* The big portion is for him. The small one for you.

MOLINA. What difference does it make?

WARDEN. You're smart maricon. Figure it out. Make sure he eats it.

MOLINA. *(As he presents to two tin plates.)* Voila, monsieur, our specialty of the evening. Flambee of merde.

(Switches plates, putting one before VALENTIN.)

VALENTIN. I have more than you do. Here, you take mine.

MOLINA. No, thank you. Eat your own.

VALENTIN. There's too much. I can't eat all of this. Why would they give me so much?

MOLINA. Maybe they're sorry they beat the shit out of you. They're making amends.

VALENTIN. Here. You eat it.

MOLINA. No.

VALENTIN. Yes, you. Eat.

MOLINA. No

VALENTIN. Yes. *(VALENTIN switches the plates. MOLINA starts to speak again. VALENTIN glares at him. MOLINA starts to eat. He takes small, tidy bites as VALENTIN shakes his head.)* Do you always eat like that?

MOLINA. You've seen me eat before.

VALENTIN. Take man bites.

MOLINA. I will take lady-like bites. I'm not an animal, like you. Lady-like bites. How does your Marta eat?

VALENTIN. *(Eating.)* I never notices. That's the last thing a man notices about a woman--how she eats!

MOLINA. If I loved someone I would notice every single thing about them. How they eat, how they sleep, everything!

VALENTIN. You're not eating.

MOLINA. Thank you for noticing. *(MOLINA picks at food, while VALENTIN eats heartily.)* Is she the only one? Don't you cheat? Wasn't there ever any other? How about the first one?

VALENTIN. Yes! No! I don't know! None of your business! What about you? Do you have someone? A fellow?

MOLINA. *(Laughs.)* I'm sorry. We don't use that word. A "fellow". I suddenly see Fred McMurray.

VALENTIN. You know what I mean.

MOLINA. *(Yes.)* His name is Gabriel. He's a waiter.

VALENTIN. You've been here three years. You must really miss him.

MOLINA. I do. But not the way you mean. We never made love.

VALENTIN. You never fucked?

MOLINA. You have a real way with words, my friend. *(We see GABRIEL in the cell.)* No, we've never touched. *(GABRIEL takes their plates away. To VALENTIN.)* It's not that I don't want to. It's him. He's married, a child. He likes me though, as a friend. That's enough. He writes me some times.

(MUSIC up. Music cue #12 "GABRIEL'S LETTER/MY FIRST WOMAN")

GABRIEL:
DEAR MOLINA...
I'M SORRY TO HEAR THEY'VE TAKEN YOU AWAY
I'M SURE YOU'RE INNOCENT.
YOU'RE SUCH A GOOD MAN
YOU MUST BE INNOCENT.

MOLINA. Thank you. Do you always take such good care of your customers?

GABRIEL:
AND I'M SORRY IF I'VE NEVER TOLD YOU HOW GRATEFUL
     I AM
FOR THE MOVIES, THE TALKS, AND THE BOOKS
THE GIFTS TO MY WIFE AND NEWBORN CHILD
I'M TRULY SORRY

MOLINA. You work so hard. Don't you have a night off?

GABRIEL:
AND FINALLY, I'M SORRY FOR ANY PAIN I MAY HAVE
     CAUSED YOU

I KNOW WHAT YOU WANTED OF ME BUT I'M JUST NOT
    THAT WAY

    MOLINA. I have an extra ticket for the ballet.

    GABRIEL:

WHAT A STRANGE THING TO BE SORRY FOR

BUT THAT'S THE WAY IT IS, ISN'T IT?

    MOLINA. Perhaps you'd like to come with me?

    GABRIEL:

I'M SORRY

SIMPLY SORRY

    MOLINA. Funny. I don't feel well. My stomach. I think I'll lie
down for a moment.

    GABRIEL:

I'M SORRY

SIMPLY SORRY

(GABRIEL helps MOLINA to his cot.)

    VALENTIN: *(Not to MOLINA, but in reverie.)*

MY FIRST WOMAN

I REMEMBER MY FIRST WOMAN

BACK OF A BUILDING

ME AND MY FRIEND

A COUPLE OF PESOS

THERE ON THE GRAVEL

DOWN ON HER KNEES

WHAT DID SHE LOOK LIKE?

PROBABLY PLAIN

WHO CAN REMEMBER

BUT TO ME SHE WAS THE KEEPER OF ALL MYSTERY.

(GABRIEL appears again.)

    GABRIEL:

AND FINALLY

I'M SORRY FOR

ANY PAIN I MAY

HAVE CAUSED YOU   **VALENTIN:**

                           MY FIRST WOMAN

                           I REMEMBER MY FIRST

                           WOMAN

GABRIEL:
I KNOW WHAT YOU WANTED
    OF ME
BUT I'M JUST NOT THAT WAY

VALENTIN:
BACK OF A BUILDING
ME AND MY FRIENDS
A COUPLE OF PESOS
THERE ON THE GRAVEL
DOWN ON HER KNEES
WHAT DID SHE LOOK LIKE?

I'M SORRY
WHAT A STRANGE THING
    TO BE SORRY FOR
BUT THAT'S THE WAY IT IS
ISN'T IT?
I'M SORRY
SIMPLY SORRY
YOUR FRIEND, GABRIEL
(He Exits.)

PROBABLY PLAIN
BUT TO ME SHE WAS
    THE KEEPER
OF ALL MYSTERY
MYSTERY.

MOLINA. *(Clutching his stomach.)* Oh!
VALENTIN. What's the matter?
MOLINA. A cramp.
VALENTIN. Take deep breaths.
MOLINA. I can't. I'm scared.
VALENTIN. No one dies from cramps.
MOLINA. Wanna bet?
VALENTIN. What can I do? Tell me what to do.
MOLINA. God, that must be hard for you to say. Get me to the hospital. Please. Please.

(VALENTIN rushes to the bars of the cell.)

VALENTIN. Guards! Guards! Molina needs to go to the infirmary!

(BLACKOUT)

Guards!

Scene 10

(Music cue #14 "MORPHINE TANGO 1")
*(The Infirmary. MOLINA is revealed on a gurney surrounded by SIX
   MEN dressed in various 'orderly' costumes.)*

ORDERLIES:
OOH...
FIRST YOU TAKE YOUR ARM AND STICK IT OUT
THEN YOU TAKE A TUBE YOU TWIST ABOUT
PULL IT TIGHT UNTIL YOU FIND A NICE, BLUE VEIN
AND OOH, OOH, OOH, OOH, OOH, OOH, OOH

THEN YOU TAKE TWO FINGERS, PAT THE SKIN
TRY THE NEEDLE OUT THEN STICK IT IN
ANY SECOND NOW, YOU'LL FEEL NO PAIN

JUST OOH, OOH, OOH, OOH, OOH, OOH, OOH, OOH

NOT BAD, IS IT?
DREAMS DRIFT BY
LOVED ONES VISIT
AS YOU LIE THERE...
OOH... OOH... OOH...

*(DANCE. Then, as the lights dim and change, the ORDERLIES de-
   part and MOLINA'S MOTHER appears.)*

MOLINA. Am I dying, Mama?
MOTHER. Hooo! Listen to him! A good son doesn't die before
his mother. You're going to see me off, thank you very much, and I'm
going to be waiting for you with a good warm shawl.
MOLINA. I'm so sick, mama.
MOTHER. A good son sees his poor old mother through her old
age; he doesn't leave her for a tummy ache!
MOLINA. You're not old. You're still beautiful.
MOTHER. I bet you say that to all the girls.
MOLINA. There are no girls, mama. I've brought you such shame.

MOTHER. No, Luis. Only if you did something cruel, uncaring. *(MUSIC. MOTHER brushes MOLINA'S hair from his forehead as if he were a little boy.):*
YOU COULD NEVER SHAME ME
THERE, I'VE TOLD YOU SO
MANY THINGS CONFUSE ME
BUT THIS I KNOW

LET THE NEIGHBORS GOSSIP
AT THE MENTION OF YOUR NAME
YOU HAVE NEVER BROUGHT ME SHAME

I KNOW SOME MAMAS HAVE ROUGHNECKS
WHO NEVER BRING THEM JOY
THANK GOD, YOU'RE NOT THAT KIND OF BOY

I KNOW THAT YOU'RE DIFFERENT
I DON'T REALLY CARE
I WOULD NEVER CHANGE A HAIR
    MOTHER. You like this Valentin, don't you?
    MOLINA. To him I'm a silly window dresser. That's all I am to everyone but you.
    MOTHER. Hoo! What nonsense. *(Continues singing):*
SOME OTHER MAMAS HAVE CHILDREN
WHOSE SECRETS HURT THEM SO
BUT YOU HAVE NO SECRETS. I ALREADY KNOW

AND YOU COULD NEVER SHAME ME
LET ME SAY OUT LOUD
I'VE A SON
A LOVING SON
WHO MAKES ME PROUD.

(The ORDERLIES reappear and conduct the MOTHER offstage, re-vealing the SPIDER WOMAN who is sitting on MOLINA's cot in the cell. The stage grows dim, and the web appears. We hear the SPIDER WOMAN'S music. MOLINA stares at her.)
(Music cue # 14B "A VISIT")

SPIDER WOMAN *(To MOLINA):*
GOOD EVENING. HOW HAVE YOU BEEN?
   MOLINA:
GO AWAY. YOU KNOW HOW I'VE BEEN.
   SPIDER WOMAN:
I ONLY WANT TO TALK WHY ARE YOU AFRAID?
   MOLINA:
I'VE ALWAYS BEEN AFRAID OF YOU!
   SPIDER WOMAN:
BUT WHY?
   MOLINA:
I DON'T KNOW.
   SPIDER WOMAN:
IT WILL CHANGE
SOMEDAY YOU'LL RECOGNIZE ME
AS YOUR FRIEND
   MOLINA:
NO, NEVER MY FRIEND, GO AWAY
   SPIDER WOMAN:
BUT I'M BEAUTIFUL
   MOLINA:
YES, YOU ARE
   SPIDER WOMAN:
AND I AM WARM AND KIND AND
GENTLE, WHY DON'T YOU LIKE ME?
   MOLINA:
I DON'T KNOW.
   SPIDER WOMAN:
SOMEDAY YOU WILL UNDERSTAND
I AM YOUR FRIEND
SOMEDAY YOU WILL KISS ME
   MOLINA:
NEVER. NEVER. GO AWAY. GO AWAY
   SPIDER WOMAN:
SOMEDAY YOU'LL GIVE IN
OF COURSE YOU WILL. ALL MEN DO.
YES, ALL MEN KISS ME AND YOU WILL TOO
YOU'LL PART MY LIPS AND REST YOURS THERE.

YOU'LL RUN YOUR FINGERS THROUGH MY HAIR
YOUR CRIES OF PLEASURE
WILL HEAT THE COOL, NIGHT AIR
WHEN YOU KISS ME
AND YOU WILL KISS ME
BUT NOT NOW! NOT YET! NOT NOW!

(She disappears. MOLINA tries to crawl back to the gurney, moaning. The ORDERLIES enter and help him back, placing him on the gurney and covering him up with a sheet.)

ORDERLIES:
OOOH!
NOW THAT YOU HAVE FOUND THIS PERFECT PLACE
PERMANENT DELIGHT LIGHTS UP YOUR FACE
NEVER MIND THE RHUMBA BEAT OF SWEET COCAINE
JUST CHANGE THIS MORBID SCENE
TAKE SOME MORE MORPHINE
AND DO, OOH, OOH, OOH, OOH
THE MORPHINE TANGO.
OOH, OOH, OOH, OOH, OOH, OOH,
OOOOOOOOOOOOHHHHHH...

(MARCOS and ESTEBAN enter and roll MOLINA off as the ORDERLIES exit and the lights fade to:)

(BLACKOUT)

Scene 11

(MOLINA, escorted by ESTEBAN and MARCOS is led into the cell.)

ESTEBAN. You won't be so lonely now, Valentin. Here's your little friend back.
  VALENTIN. *(To MOLINA.)* How are you?
  MOLINA. Still a little woozy. So, if I stumble over the line, you'll understand
  MARCOS. Hey, Valentin, look what else we brought you. A

special meal. Beans with pork. The Warden's in good spirits. Your friend, the one with the bag over his head, told us everything we wanted to know.

VALENTIN. I don't believe you.

(VALENTIN reaches for the food.)

MARCOS. *(Holding it back.)* Say please.

VALENTIN. Go to hell.

ESTEBAN. Big words for someone who hasn't eaten in three days.

(VALENTIN takes the plate and starts wolfing down the food.)

MARCOS. That's disgusting.

ESTEBAN. C'mon, Marcos, let's leave them alone. Homos reunion.

(ESTEBAN and MARCOS exit. VALENTIN continues to devour food greedily as MOLINA sits and watches him.)

VALENTIN. The first food they've given me in days. I was beginning to think they were trying to starve me to death.

MOLINA. Not so fast. Look what happened to me.

VALENTIN. You want to hear something crazy? It's not half bad. I must be cracking up. How was the infirmary?

MOLINA. Males nurses and morphine! I loved it. Did you miss me?

VALENTIN. As a matter of fact, I did.

MOLINA. Now don't get any funny ideas. How did you spend your time? Thinking about Marta?

VALENTIN. It's driving me crazy. If she's sleeping with someone else I'll kill her, then him, with my bare hands.

MOLINA. That will be a nice getting-out-of-prison surprise for both of them. I'm sure she's spending all her time making bombs for the revolution anyway!

VALENTIN. We don't make bombs.

MOLINA. All right, stuffing envelopes then.

VALENTIN. Marta's not in the movement.

MOLINA. What new twist is this?

VALENTIN. I have a confession to make. She's upper class, drives a little red Mercedes, 180 SL, and plays golf.

MOLINA. She sounds divine. Does she have a brother?

VALENTIN. She's everything Golizar says we're supposed to hate and I'm crazy about her.

MOLINA. Golizar? Alberto Golizar? That Golizar?

VALENTIN. Don't ell me you've heard of him.

MOLINA. I don't just read movie magazines. He's a great man.

VALENTIN. He changed my life. I didn't know there was another way until him. I was seventeen years old when I heard him speak. There were thousands of people. He made us feel like one. He opened our eyes, our minds, our hearts, Molina. It's funny how your life can change forever in an instant.

MOLINA. No, it's not, Valentin.

VALENTIN. The man next to me was hiding a gun. There were plain clothes police everywhere awaiting orders to open fire. It was a massacre. I never went back to my village. I slept in the streets. I stole. I got arrested. I joined the movement.

MOLINA. Please don't tell me any more.

VALENTIN. I started out just being Señor Golizar's personal bodyguard.

MOLINA. I don't want to know.

VALENTIN. Now, I'm in charge of getting fugitives... Oh, God!

MOLINA. What's wrong?

VALENTIN. *(Falling to his knees.)* My stomach! Such cramps! Something in the food! I've never felt such pain. No, oh Jesus God, no!

MOLINA. What happened?

VALENTIN. I'm so ashamed.

MOLINA. Ashamed. Why?

VALENTIN. I shit myself.

MOLINA. Stay there.

(MOLINA leaves VALENTIN on the cell floor to get some things from the sink area.)

VALENTIN. What are you doing?

MOLINA. We'll clean you up.

VALENTIN. My God! The food. The cramps. I've been poisoned just like you were.

MOLINA. Don't talk, come on, help.

(MOLINA pulls VALENTIN'S trousers and soiled underpants off, takes the soiled clothing behind the cloth curtain that partitions off the lavatory area, and returns with a wash cloth and begins to wipe off VALENTIN'S legs.)

VALENTIN. This doesn't disgust you?

MOLINA. I don't want to make a career of it. Open your thighs.

VALENTIN. I feel like a little boy.

MOLINA. You don't look like one. Raise your hips.

(He goes to the basin with the wash cloth. A GUARD passes by the cell.)

GUARD. Anything wrong?

MOLINA. Nothing.

GUARD. What are you doing in there?

MOLINA. What do you think we're doing? Please!

(GUARD makes a sound/gesture of contempt and moves on. MOLINA slides a clean pair of pants onto VALENTIN and helps him to his cot.)

VALENTIN. You're a character.

MOLINA. And you're not?

VALENTIN. You're a kind man, Molina. (He shudders.) Marta!

(VALENTIN faints.)

MOLINA. *(Sung to VALENTIN.):*
SHE WEARS SATIN
SPANISH LACE
SHE FEELS WILD CHINCHILLA
BRUSH ACROSS HER FACE.

SHE'S LUCKY
SHE'S A WOMAN

SHE WEARS DIAMONDS
BRIGHT AS STARS
SHE HAS LOVERS OPEN DOORS
TO FANCY CARS
SHE'S LUCKY
SO LUCKY
SHE'S A WOMAN

A PERFUME BY LANVIN
TO DAB ACROSS HER WRIST
A SECRET, RIBBONED DIARY
OF ALL THE MEN SHE'S KISSED
SO MANY MEN SHE'S KISSED

LILAC WATERS
BATHE HER SKIN
AT THE OPERA, USHERS GASP
WHEN SHE SWEEPS IN
GIFTS OF CHOCOLATE
ROSES TOO
HAND DELIVERED NOTES
CONFESSING "I LOVE YOU"
MILKY LOTIONS
SCENTED CREAMS
SHE'S THE CLIMAX OF YOUR TECHNICOLOR DREAMS

HOW LUCKY CAN YOU BE?
SO LUCKY, YOU'LL AGREE
AND I WISH THAT SHE WERE ME
THAT
WOMAN!

WARDEN. Hello, Molina. Did you think I'd forgotten you?
(Music cue #15 "SPIDER WOMAN UNDERSCORE")
MOLINA. I don't have anything for you yet. He's very suspicious. I just need time. I lost nearly a week when I was in the infirmary.

I just need time. I lost nearly a week when I was in the infirmary. He took the wrong plate. I nearly died. How is she?

WARDEN. Who?

MOLINA. My mother! You said if I cooperated with you I would be released for good behavior.

WARDEN. Did I? I don't remember.

MOLINA. We made a deal.

WARDEN. Then keep your end of it.

MOLINA. I'm not the person for this. I'm not political. I don't know about these things. I don't care about them.

WARDEN. That's exactly why I'm counting on you.

MOLINA. He told me he's willing to die for his cause.

WARDEN. And you're willing to betray him for yours.

MOLINA. I don't have a cause. I have a mother who needs me.

WARDEN. The sooner her talks, the sooner you'll be free to walk out of here and be with her.

(VALENTIN stirs. MOLINA is mopping VALENTIN'S brow and soothing him.)

VALENTIN. I'm so cold.

MOLINA. I'll get you a blanket. *(Suddenly, the SPIDER WOMAN opens the cell curtains.)* No!

VALENTIN. What's happening to me Molina?

MOLINA. The food. You've been poisoned.

VALENTIN. The pain! I can't take this. Get me to the infirmary.

MOLINA. No! It's what they want.

VALENTIN. Please!

MOLINA. They'll give you morphine. You'll talk. *(VALENTIN clutches his stomach in pain.)* Valentin, think of Aurora. *See* her!

VALENTIN. I can't.

MOLINA. What movie was I telling you? Help me, Valentin!

WARDEN. What are you doing, Molina?

MOLINA. He likes me to tell him movies.

WARDEN. I want him in the infirmary.

MOLINA. I'll get your names, goddamnit! Now please, go away, leave us alone!

WARDEN. Are you falling in love with him, Molina?

MOLINA. Darling, I like minors, remember? He'll talk.

WARDEN. If he doesn't, you can forget all about ever seeing your mother again. You're right to worry about her, Molina. She's dying.

(Lights down on WARDEN.)

VALENTIN. I'm dying, Molina.

MOLINA. You're not. I won't let you. Now, what movie (BIRDS start.) were we in? I can't think. There were so many!

VALENTIN. Aurora's been taken prisoner.

MOLINA. I know where I am now, BIRD OF PARADISE! The night-club scene. She is so tremendous in this sequence. You remembered Valentin! *(Drums start.)* Her lover has escaped. She alone knows where he is.

VALENTIN. Will she betray him?

MOLINA. She tries to pretend *(Vocals start)* that it is not her concern what happens in this world for good or evil.

VALENTIN. But she can't do it. She does care.

MOLINA. Yes, Valentin, she is only a woman who loves! Let them kill her even. She will not betray the man she loves.

(MUSIC up. AURORA and dancers enter. AURORA is in a cage.)

*(SONG: **Music cue #16 "LET'S MAKE LOVE"**)*

Scene 12

(The scene changes and we are back in MOLINA'S movie. MALE DANCERS are seen upstage.)

MEN:

GIMME LOVE, GIMME LOVE, GIMME KISSES, GIMME LOVE
GIMME LOVE, GIMME KISSES, GIMMME LOVE, LOVE, LOVE
GIMME LOVE, GIMME LOVE, GIMME KISSES, GIMME LOVE
GIMME LOVE, GIMME KISSES, GIMME LOVE, LOVE, LOVE

GIMME LOVE, GIMME KISSES, GIMME KISSES, GIMME LOVE
GIMME LOVE, GIMME KISSES, GIMME LOVE, LOVE, LOVE

(AURORA appears.)

AURORA:
IF THERE'S A WAR ON, DON'T BRING ME THE NEWS
ASK ME TO BULL FIGHTS AND I MUST REFUSE
BUT IF YOU WANT TO GET MY ATTENTION
LET'S MAKE LOVE
    MEN:
GIMME LOVE, GIMME KISSES, GIMME LOVE
GIMME LOVE, GIMME KISSES, GIMME LOVE
    AURORA:
IF THERE'S AN EARTHQUAKE I WILL NOT ATTEND
    MEN:
GIMME KISSES, GIMME LOVE
    AURORA:
IF THERE'S A PLAGUE DON'T INVITE ME MY FRIEND
    MEN:
GIMME KISSES, GIMME LOVE, LOVE, LOVE
    AURORA:
BUT IF YOU WANT TO KEEP ME LOOKING IN YOUR
            DIRECTION
LET'S MAKE LOVE
    MEN:
GIMME LOVE, GIMME KISSES; GIMME LOVE
GIMME LOVE, GIMME KISSES, GIMME LOVE, LOVE, LOVE
GIMME LOVE, GIMME LOVE, GIMME KISSES, GIMME LOVE,
GIMME LOVE, GIMME KISSES, GIMME LOVE

AURORA:	MEN:
IT'S LIKE GIVING TO THE NEEDY	OOH, AH, UH
AND I DON'T MIND BEING GREEDY.	OOH, AH, UH, UH
COME ON, CHICO, PLEASE BE SPEEDY	
AND BRING ME WHAT I LONG FOR	OOH

(Dance Break.)

AURORA:
IF THERE'S A FIRE DON'T BRING ME A HOSE
  MEN:
GIMME KISSES, GIMME LOVE
  AURORA:
CALL ME A COWARD, THAT'S TRUE, I SUPPOSE
  MEN:
GIMME LOVE, LOVE, KISSES, GIMME LOVE
  AURORA:
BUT ALL I WANT IS BEAUTY
SO,

MEN:	**AURORA:**
GIMME, GIMME, GIMME GIMEE	HUGS
GIMME, GIMME, GIMME, GIMME	SQUEEZES
GIMME, GIMME, GIMME, GIMME	LIPS
GIMME, GIMME, GIMME, GIMME	KISSES

  AURORA:
SO LET'S NOT MAKE MORE TROUBLE
LET'S MAKE LOVE

MEN:	**AURORA:**
GIMME LOVE	KISS
GIMME GIMME LOVE, LOVE, LOVE	KISS
GIMME, GIMME, GIMME, LOVE, LOVE	KISS
GIMME, LOVE, LOVE	KISS KISS
GIMME, GIMME, GIMME GIMME	
GIMME, GIMME, GIMME, GIMME	
GIMME, GIMME, GIMME, LOVE	

*(DANCE. Suddenly, the music and movement become nervous, anx-
ious. AURORA is enclosed within her cage. MOLINA rushes towards the cell. MARCOS runs his nightstick across the bars as
the MUSIC Stops. The movie freezes. Lights on the cell as MOLINA
rips the blanket off of VALENTIN.)*

MOLINA. The guards. They're coming. You've got to get up. Otherwise they'll take you away.

(ESTEBAN and MARCOS enter.)

MARCOS. Good evening.

ESTEBAN. Good evening, Molina. Good evening, Valentin. We hear you're sick. We've come to take you to the infirmary.

MOLINA. Sick? I don't know what you're talking about. He's fine.

VALENTIN. I'm fine.

MOLINA. *(Aside to GUARDS.)* Don't take him now. He's about to talk. I just got his girlfriend's name.

ESTEBAN. What is it?

MOLINA. Betty.

ESTEBAN. What kind of a name is Betty for a Latin girl?

MOLINA. I'll pry a little deeper. Maybe she's Swiss.

MARCOS. The warden won't like this, Molina.

MOLINA. Fuck the warden.

(The GUARDS exit. The moment they are gone, VALENTIN collapses. Movie returns to life.)
*(**Music cue #16A ACT I—CURTAIN**)*

MEN:
GIMME LOVE, GIMME LOVE, GIMME KISSES, GIMME LOVE
GIMME LOVE, GIMME KISSES, GIMME LOVE, LOVE, LOVE
GIMME LOVE, GIMME LOVE, GIMME KISSES, GIMME LOVE
GIMME LOVE, GIMME KISSES, GIMME LOVE, LOVE, LOVE

(MOLINA opens the curtain. The SPIDER WOMAN is gone. VALENTIN faints. MOLINA catches him in his arms.)

MOLINA. She's gone. You're safe. Thank God, you're safe. Come with me.

(MOLINA carries him into his movie. Bird calls swell up again suddenly.)

BLACKOUT

CURTAIN

END OF ACT I

ACT II

Scene 1

(Music Cue # 17 ENTR'ACTE.)

PRISONERS:
AH-UH AH-UH
AH-UH AH-UH
   SPIDER WOMAN *(V.O.):*
SOONER OR LATER
YOUR LOVE WILL ARRIVE
AND SHE TOUCHES YOUR HEART
YOU'RE ALERT, YOU'RE ALIVE
AND THERE'S ONLY ONE PIN THAT CAN PUNCTURE SUCH
   BLISS
HER KISS
   MOLINA. Picnic in Rio! You're lucky you have a window dresser for a cellmate. You could be living with a homosexual.
   VALENTIN. Molina, I want you to give your mother a message for me. Tell her this is the best fucking chicken I've ever eaten.
   MOLINA. She'll be delighted to hear that, I'm sure. *(VALENTIN burps.)* That's lovely.
   VALENTIN. I just did it to get your goat. You know what I feel like? One of your movies. I know just the one, too.
   MOLINA. You're hooked.
   VALENTIN. I'm not hooked.
   MOLINA. He's hooked.
   VALENTIN. All right, maybe I am a little bit!
   MOLINA. Which one?
   VALENTIN. To save her lover, Aurora agrees to marry a man she doesn't love on the eve of the Russian Revolution.
   MOLINA. *(Through bars.)* HE'S HOOKED!
   VALENTIN. Of course I'm hooked. You don't get this sort of thing in dialectical materialism. Please, Molina.
   MOLINA. FLAME OF ST. PETERSBURG, the final reel.
   VALENTIN. Thank you.

(VALENTIN listens eagerly.)

MOLINA. Tatyana Alexandrovna, vedette du cabaret, is singing her final number. *(MUSIC offstage. **Music cue #18 "GOOD TIMES".** AURORA is heard singing. MUSIC continues under following narration.)* All St. Petersburg is there. The Tsar himself is in the audience. It is her farewell performance. Tomorrow she will be the Countess Ostrovsky.

(AURORA begins to sing.)

AURORA:
THERE'S GOING TO BE GOOD TIMES
NOTHING BUT GOOD TIMES
THEY'RE GOING TO BE SCATTERING THOSE CLOUDS OF
          GRAY

AND ALL OF THOSE BAD TIMES
THOSE TERRIBLE BAD TIMES
ARE GOING TO BE PACKING UP AND LEAVING TOWN
          TODAY

SO PUT ON A SMILE
START WAVING YOUR HAND
WHATEVER WAS GRIM IS GOING TO BE GRANT
AND...

(AURORA encourages the company to join her.)

THERE'S GOING TO BE GOOD TIMES
NOTHING BUT GOOD TIMES

(AURORA cuts off company and finishes song.)

GOOD TIMES ARE COMING YOUR WAY

MOLINA. The number ends. Pandemonium. *(Offstage we hear "bravos!" and applause.)* They don't want to let her go. A student leaps from the balcony to show his devotion.

COMPANY. *(Offstage.)* Ah!

(AURORA crosses the stage.)

MOLINA. Cut to her dressing room and her faithful maid, Lisette.
AURORA. Oh, how they love me! Listen! If only (I only wish) I loved the man I am pledged to wed.

(Musical underscoring begins.)

MOLINA. "Madame."
AURORA. Yes, Lisette?
MOLINA. "A note arrived for you".

(MOLINA "hands" a note to AURORA who "reads" it.)

AURORA. "County Ostrovsky has deceived you. Your lover, the student revolutionary Bolshevik anarchist, Anatol, will be shot as he waits for you in vain on the Pushkin bridge this evening at the stroke of midnight. Signed, A friend." I must save him. Summon my troika.
MOLINA. " But, madame, the danger—!"
AURORA. Not a word, (Lisette). Pas un mot!

(Musical underscoring stops abruptly.)

MOLINA. *(To VALENTIN.)* Well-bred Russians often spoke French among themselves.
VALENTIN. I knew that.
MOLINA. No, you didn't.
VALENTIN. All right, I didn't.

(Musical underscoring begins again.)

AURORA. To be in love is the sweetest thing, Lisette. But to risk everything for love is even sweeter!

(VOICES are heard offstage clamoring for Tatyana. Actors appear including WARDEN pounding on dressing room door.)

ONE VOICE. *(WARDEN.)* Tatyana, my love!

OTHERS. Tatiana! My diva! Tatiana!

AURORA. *(With loathing.)* C'est lui, Ostrovsky!

MOLINA. "How you hate him!"

AURORA. Oh, God!

VOICE. My carriage is waiting, my love!

AURORA. Quick. There's not time. I'll slip out the back way. Hold him at bay just as long as you can.

VOICE. Tatiana!

AURORA. Adieu, Lisette. Courage.

VOICE. Tatiana!!!

(AURORA exits, as does "OSTROVSKY" and OTHERS.)

MOLINA. Cut to dark shadowy streets. Snow is falling. *(AURORA re-enters.)* The wind whistles. A night of terror. The clock strikes midnight. *(A Bell sounds.)* Tatyana dismisses her troika driver. As she hurries down the empty, terrifying, night-shadowed streets, her whole life swirls before her. At last she sees the little bridge over the canal and in the light of its solitary streetlamp, her lover. She is in time. She will save him. They will flee to Paris. She begins to run but his figure seems to recede. It is like a terrible dream.

AURORA *(Singing):*
ANATOL!

MOLINA. He turns. His eyes light up. He calls to her.

VALENTIN *(Singing):*
"TATYANA!"

MOLINA. Bang. Close-up. Joy, not pain illuminates her features. Courage, not fear is writ large across her face. This is not death. This is ecstasy.

AURORA. Anatol, my Anatol. I wanted to warn you.

VALENTIN. "What have you done for me, my Tatyana?"

AURORA. Nothing, nothing, my Anatol!

(AURORA slowly falls to the ground.)

MOLINA. Red blood stains the snowy street. She is fading fast. She is in her lover's arms at last, again, and somehow forever. *(AURORA sings.)*

AURORA:
SO PUT ON A SMILE
START WAVING YOUR HAND
WHATEVER WAS GRIM IS GOING TO BE GRAND

(She appears to die. Then she suddenly rises again.)

AND—

THERE'S GOING TO BE GOOD TIMES
NOTHING BUT GOOD TIMES
VIVA LA GUERRA, VIVA LA REVOLUCION, VIVA—!

(AURORA dies.)

VALENTIN. (Speak-singing.)
GOOD TIMES ARE COMING OUR WAY...

(The vision of AURORA fades. The two men are silent a moment, touched by what has happened.)

MOLINA. Fade to black. The end. There's not a dry eye in the house.
VALENTIN. You know, Molina...
MOLINA. Except one!
VALENTIN. You know there's one thing profoundly wrong about your movies, don't you?
MOLINA. What is that, doctor?
VALENTIN. They're not real.
MOLINA. Thank you. Of course they're not real. They're better than real. I need my movies to remind me that there can be beauty and grace and bravery and loyalty and kindness and love and yes, dumb jokes and singing and dancing and Technicolor and happy endings even and love. I already said that.
VALENTIN. Why don't you try to find them in your own life?
MOLINA. I have tried. I failed. I am not a stupid man, Valentin.
VALENTIN. I guess I have a movie, too.
MOLINA. I hope you do, my friend.
VALENTIN. Only there's no part in mine for your Aurora. No singing, no dancing, no pretty costumes. Just the truth.

VALENTIN:
IT WAS MADE OUT OF MUD
AND PIECES OF TIN
AND BOXES NAILED TOGETHER
CARDBOARD BOXES
MY CASTLE
MY HOME

AND WE SLEPT ON THE FLOOR
MY SISTER AND I
WITH GUNNY SACKS FOR OUR PILLOWS
COUGHING, HUNGRY
COZY
MY HOME

AND EVERY SUNDAY
ON OUR KNEES
WE WOULD THANK THE LORD
FOR HIS BOUNTIFUL BLESSINGS

AND OUR MOTHER POURED SOUP
INTO LITTLE CRACKED BOWLS
AS SHE SPOKE OF SOMETHING BETTER
BEEF STEAK, MAYBE, SOMEDAY
MY HOME

AND THAT LADY HAD EYES
THAT WERE EMPTY AND COLD
AT THE RIPE OLD AGE OF THIRTY
DEATH CAME
WELCOME
TO MY HOME.

AND STILL THAT SUNDAY
ON OUR KNEES
HOW WE THANKED THE LORD
FOR HIS BOUNTIFUL BLESSINGS

AND MY SISTER AND I
SWORE THE DAY THAT WE LEFT
THERE'D BE NO MORE CHILDREN LIKE US
IN THE FILTH THERE, IN THE HEAT THERE, IN THE SMELL
     THERE

AND NO MORE SUNDAYS
ON OUR KNEES
WOULD WE THANK THE LORD
FOR HIS BOUNTIFUL BLESSINGS

AND WE CAME TO THE CITY
AND BEGGED FOR OUR FOOD
THEN, ONE APRIL DAY WE HEARD IT
THUNDER RUMBLING
ONE MAN SPEAKING
THOUSANDS   SINGING...

SOMEDAY WE'LL BE FREE
I PROMISE YOU, WE'LL BE FREE
IF NOT TOMORROW
THEN THE DAY AFTER THAT

AND THE CANDLES IN OUR HAND
WILL ILLUMINATE THIS LAND,
IF NOT TOMORROW,
THEN THE DAY AFTER THAT

AND THE WORLD THAT GIVES US PAIN
THAT FILLS OUR LIVES WITH FEAR
ON THE DAY AFTER THAT WILL DISAPPEAR

AND THE WAR WE'VE FOUGHT TO WIN
I PROMISE YOU WE WILL WIN
IF NOT TOMORROW
THEN THE DAY AFTER THAT
OR THE DAY AFTER THAT

CHORUS:	**VALENTIN:**
SOMEDAY WE'LL BE FREE	
I PROMISE YOU, WE'LL BE FREE	
IF NOT TOMORROW	IF NOT TOMORROW
THEN THE DAY AFTER THAT OR THE	
DAY AFTER THAT	
AND THE CANDLES IN OUR HAND	
WILL ILLUMINATE THIS LAND	
IF NOT TOMORROW	IF NOT TOMORROW
THEN THE DAY AFTER THAT OR THE	
DAY AFTER THAT	
AND THE WORLD THAT GIVES US PAIN	
THAT FILLS OUR LIVES WITH FEAR	
ON THE DAY AFTER THAT	
WILL DISAPPEAR	WILL DISAPPEAR

VALENTIN and CHORUS:
WILL DISAPPEAR

AND THE WAR WE'VE FOUGHT TO WIN
I PROMISE YOU WE WILL WIN
IF NOT TOMORROW
THEN THE DAY AFTER THAT
OR THE DAY AFTER THAT
OR THE DAY AFTER THAT
OR THE DAY AFTER THAT
OR THE DAY AFTER THAT

OR THE DAY
AFTER THAT!

*(A musical discordant sound we have heard before--when a PRIS-
ONER was dragged throughout the prison--sounds again.
ESTEBAN and MARCOS enter, dragging a PRISONER with a
bag over his head. They stop in front of the cell.)*

ESTEBAN. *(To VALENTIN.)* Recognize your old friend, Valentin?

(ESTEBAN rips the bag off the PRISONER'S head and pulls his head back by the hair. VALENTIN shakes his head "no" and turns away.)

VALENTIN. I've never seen him before.

MARCOS. *(Putting bag back on.)* Some friend, eh? Back we go amigo.

MOLINA. You goddamn murdering bastards.

ESTEBAN. You better warn your little maricon, Valentin. Those were big words.

MARCOS. They might cost him.

(MARCOS and ESTEBAN exit with PRISONER.)

VALENTIN. That was dumb.

MOLINA. Dumb and dizzy. That's me all over, darling.

VALENTIN. That's not true.

MOLINA. You're a bad influence. Will you stop trying to make a man out of me?

VALENTIN. *(Almost despite himself.)* That prisoner was him, Molina. The one I got the passport to. One of the names they want from me.

MOLINA. Please--I don't want to hear!

VALENTIN. Sweet Jesus, just let it be fast when it's my time.

MOLINA. Don't say that. Don't even think it!

(MOLINA goes to VALENTIN and puts his hand on his shoulder.)

VALENTIN. You better go back to your side.

(BLACKOUT)

Scene 2

(Music cue # 20A "PRISON UNDERSCORE 3")
(MOLINA'S MOTHER appears in her usher's uniform--in Limbo.)

MOTHER. Luis! Are you going shopping? I need some things.

Some guava paste.

(MOLINA appears--in Limbo.)

MOLINA. I need some guava paste this time.
MOTHER. Some sugar.
MOLINA. A large bag of sugar.
MOTHER. Two boxes of tea.
MOLINA. Two boxes of tea.
MOTHER. Both camomile.
MOLINA. One regular and the other camomile.
MOTHER. I know how you like camomile.
MOLINA. He doesn't like camomile. Wouldn't you know?
MOTHER. Some milk.
MOLINA. And powdered milk. He goes through that like there's
no tomorrow. And I need more chicken.
MOTHER. And I thought maybe a chicken.
MOLINA. He likes my mother's chicken.
MOTHER. *(Moving off.)* I know you love my chicken.

(The MOTHER has gone.)

MARCOS. Don't write "his mother's chicken." It's not his mother's
chicken. It's ours.

*(Lights up on WARDEN's office. WARDEN, MARCOS and ESTEBAN
are interrogating MOLINA.)*

MOLINA. And where were my movie magazines?
WARDEN. I'm getting impatient, Molina.
MOLINA. What are you talking about? It's only been a month.
Men like that are very suspicious. Just give me a little more time.
WARDEN. I don't have a little more time. I don't think you have
a little more time, Molina.
MOLINA. What do you mean?
WARDEN. Your mother. She's very bad.
MOLINA. How bad?
WARDEN. Would you like to speak with her?

MOLINA. You know how much I would.

WARDEN. It's against every regulation. *(Takes the phone off the hook.)* Would you like a little privacy? *(To ESTEBAN.)* Get his supplies. The best shops.

(ESTEBAN exits.)

MOLINA. Thank you.

(Music cue #21 "MAMA, IT'S ME")
(The WARDEN hands MOLINA the phone. He starts to exit.)

MARCOS. (To the WARDEN moving upstage.) I don't understand.

WARDEN. You will.

MOLINA:
MAMA? IT'S ME
MAMA, I'M COMING TO GET YOU
IT WON'T BE MUCH LONGER
MAMA, YOU'LL SEE
BUT DON'T TRY TO TALK NOW
YOU'VE GOT TO GET STRONGER

SOON, WE'LL BE GOING TO MOVIES
I'LL BUY YOU BEAUTIFUL THINGS
WAIT TILL YOU SEE WHAT TOMORROW BRINGS...

HAPPINESS, MAMA
YOU NEVER KNOW WHERE IT MIGHT BE
MAMA, IT'S ME. IT'S ME

(MUSIC as MOLINA listens.)

HUSH, MAMA, HUSH
YOU'VE NO REASON TO CRY
NO, MAMA, NO
GOODBYE, GOODBYE

(The WARDEN moves downstage and presses the receiver button,

cutting off the call as the music ends.)

Goodbye. *(Long pause.)* I'll get the names. But not because I give a
shit about you or your stupid games.

    WARDEN. Not stupid, my friend. Very real.

    MOLINA. So is taking care of my mother. What if he doesn't
talk?

    WARDEN. He will.. Tell him you're getting out in the morning--
for good behavior. Ask him if there's anything you can do for him on
the outside. *(Another pause.)* There's the door to freedom and your
mother. You have the key to open it.

(The WARDEN exits.)

    MOLINA *(He sings):*
SOON WE'LL BE GOING TO MOVIES,
I'LL BUY YOU BEAUTIFUL THINGS.
WAIT TILL YOU SEE WHAT TOMORROW BRINGS.

(ESTEBAN enters.)

HAPPINESS MAMA,
YOU NEVER KNOW WHERE IT MIGHT BE.

(ESTEBAN turns MOLINA around to leave...)

          (BLACKOUT)

          Scene 3

The Cell

*(MOLINA is cleaning up after another "sumptuous" meal, only this
   time there are wine bottles and glasses too. VALENTIN has gorged
   himself. He almost seems, for the first time all evening, happy.)*

VALENTIN. Maybe it's this wine, but I don't feel the weight of the world on my shoulders for a change. It feels good.

MOLINA. Leave it to Mama to smuggle in a couple of bottles of my favorite red. You're probably going to miss her more than you're going too miss me.

VALENTIN. Why? Are you planning on taking a vacation?

MOLINA. I was going to tell you. I just didn't know how to break it to you. I'm getting out in the morning. Good behavior. My mother found a new attorney who went through some court of appeals...

VALENTIN. Congratulations.

MOLINA. Believe me, no one is more surprised than I am.

VALENTIN. I'm very happy for you.

MOLINA. I thought I'd [I wanted to] wait till morning to tell you. I hate long goodbyes. I hate *any* goodbyes.

VALENTIN. I'll miss you.

MOLINA. It's mutual.

VALENTIN. No, I'll really, really, miss you. I'll miss your house-keeping, I'll miss your chatter, I'll even miss Aurora and those movies.

MOLINA. Well, I wanted to put off telling you 'till tomorrow. But I always run off at the mouth, don't I?

VALENTIN. Dumb and dizzy, that's you.

MOLINA. Go to hell. I can call myself that, but you, sir, are not allowed. *(Moving towards him.)* Oops! *(Indicating the floor.)* I've crossed the line.

VALENTIN. *(Strangely serious.)* Let's forget about the line.

MOLINA. I hate feelings sometimes. Life is difficult enough.

VALENTIN. Our feelings are the only things that keep us from giving in to those bastards. You're leaving... my feelings for you aren't.

MOLINA. Thank you.

VALENTIN. Listen, Molina. When you get outside, there are a few phone calls you could make for me... I really need...

MOLINA. *(Holding his hands over his ears.)* Please! I don't want to hear.

VALENTIN. There's nothing to it. You won't be in any danger.

MOLINA. *(Louder than before.)* Please!

VALENTIN. Molina, it would mean so much to me! Only a few...

MOLINA. Please! Please!

(Music cue #22 "ANYTHING FOR HIM")
(We hear the SPIDER WOMAN'S music. She appears. She paces provocatively above the two men as the music begins. She sings.)

SPIDER WOMAN:
SOON, I FEEL IT
SOON, SOMEHOW.
I WILL HAVE HIM
ANY MINUTE NOW

MOLINA:
I'D DO ANYTHING FOR HIM.
HE MUST KNOW.
I'D DO ANYTHING FOR HIM.
I WANT HIM SO.
I'VE NO INTEREST IN HIS CAUSE.
LET THAT BE.
PLEASE, GOD, LET HIM TURN AROUND
AND LOOK AT ME.

VALENTIN:
HE'D DO ANYTHING FOR ME
I CAN TELL.
HE'D DO ANYTHING FOR ME
I KNOW HIM WELL
IF WE TOUCH BEFORE HE
    GOES
HE'LL MAKE THAT CALL.
HE'D DO ANYTHING FOR ME.
ANYTHING AT ALL.

SPIDER WOMAN:
SOON, I FEEL IT
SOON, SOMEHOW
I WILL HAVE HIM
ANY MINUTE NOW

MOLINA:	**VALENTIN:**
I'D DO ANYTHING FOR HIM.	HE'D DO ANYTHING FOR ME
HE MUST KNOW.	I CAN TELL.
I'D DO ANYTHING FOR HIM.	HE'D DO ANYTHING FOR ME.
I WANT HIM SO.	I KNOW HIM WELL.
I'D DO ANYTHING FOR HIM	IF WE TOUCH BEFORE HE
	GOES

MOLINA (cont.):
LARGE OR SMALL
I'D DO ANYTHING FOR HIM
ANYTHING AT ALL
ANYTHING AT ALL.

VALENTIN (cont.):
HE'LL MAKE THAT CALL.
HE'D DO ANYTHING FOR ME.
ANYTHING AT ALL.

(MOLINA, VALENTIN and the SPIDER WOMAN sing together.)

SPIDER WOMAN:
SOON, I FEEL IT
SOON, SOMEHOW
I WILL HAVE HIM
ANY MINUTE NOW

MOLINA:
I'D DO ANYTHING FOR HIM
HE MUST KNOW.
I'D DO ANYTHING FOR HIM
I WANT HIM SO.
I'D DO ANYTHING FOR HIM.

LARGE OR SMALL
I'D DO ANYTHING FOR HIM
ANYTHING AT ALL
ANYTHING AT ALL.

VALENTIN:
HE'D DO ANYTHING FOR ME.
I CAN TELL.
HE'D DO ANYTHING FOR ME.
I KNOW HIM WELL.
IF WE TOUCH BEFORE HE
    GOES
HE'LL MAKE THAT CALL.
HE'D DO ANYTHING FOR ME.
ANYTHING AT ALL.

(MOLINA is sitting dejectedly on his cot. The music continues under the following dialogue.)

VALENTIN. *(Coming behind MOLINA and putting his hand on MOLINA'S shoulder. He lets his hand rest on MOLINA's neck.)* Molina.

MOLINA. Please, don't... I don't want your pity. It only makes it worse.

VALENTIN. It's not pity.

(VALENTIN'S hand slides under MOLINA'S shirt.)

MOLINA. Why are you doing this?

VALENTIN. I want to.

MOLINA. Can I touch you too? *(VALENTIN nods. MOLINA slowly raises his hand and touches VALENTIN's face.)* How I've longed to do that. I've always longed to do that.

VALENTIN. Now you can. But you don't have to talk.

MOLINA. I want to tell you so many things.

VALENTIN. Jesus, I never knew anybody who liked to talk so much.

(VALENTIN blows out the candle, closes the curtains and removes his shirt. Embarrassed, MOLINA looks away.)

VALENTIN. Molina.

MOLINA. Valentin, if you like, you can do whatever you want with me... because I want you to. *(VALENTIN puts his hand out to MOLINA, who is still shy, and draws MOLINA to him.)* The nicest thing about being happy is that you never think you'll be unhappy again.

VALENTIN. This time, maybe you won't be.

(VALENTIN draws MOLINA towards him on the bed.)

(LIGHTS DOWN SLOWLY.)

Scene 4

(Music cue # 23 "KISS OF THE SPIDER WOMAN")
(The SPIDER WOMAN'S theme music as she appears isolated on the stage.)

SPIDER WOMAN:
SOONER OR LATER
YOU'RE CERTAIN TO MEET
IN THE BEDROOM, THE PARLOR OR EVEN THE STREET
THERE'S NOWHERE ON EARTH

SPIDER WOMAN (cont.):
YOU'RE LIKELY TO MISS
HER KISS

SOONER OR LATER
IN SUNLIGHT OR GLOOM
WHEN THE RED CANDLES FLICKER
SHE'LL WALK IN THE ROOM
AND THE CURTAINS WILL SHAKE AND THE FIRE WILL HISS
HERE COMES HER KISS

AND THE MOON GROWS DIMMER
AT THE TIDE'S LOW EBB
AND HER BLACK BEADS SHIMMER
AND YOU'RE ACHING TO MOVE BUT YOU'RE CAUGHT IN
        THE WEB
OF THE SPIDER WOMAN
IN HER VELVET CAPE
YOU CAN SCREAM
BUT YOU CANNOT ESCAPE

SOONER OR LATER
YOUR LOVE WILL ARRIVE
AND HE TOUCHES YOUR HEART
YOU'RE ALERT, YOU'RE ALIVE
BUT THERE'S ONLY ONE PIN THAT CAN PUNCTURE SUCH
        BLISS
HER KISS
SOONER OR LATER
YOU BATHE IN SUCCESS
AND YOUR MINIONS SALUTE
THEY SAY NOTHING BUT "YES"
BUT YOUR POWER IS EMPTY, IT FADES LIKE THE MIST
ONCE YOU'VE BEEN KISSED

AND THE MOON GROWS DIMMER
AT THE TIDE'S LOW EBB
AND YOUR BREATH COMES FASTER

SPIDER WOMAN (Cont.):
AND YOU'RE ACHING TO MOVE BUT YOU'RE CAUGHT IN
    THE WEB
OF THE SPIDER WOMAN
IN HER VELVET CAPE
YOU CAN RUN
YOU CAN SCREAM
YOU CAN HIDE
BUT YOU CANNOT ESCAPE!

(BLACKOUT)

Scene 5

(Music cue #23A "AFTER SPIDER WOMAN")
The Cell

*(MOLINA is finished packing up. He has a small cardboard suit-
    case. VALENTIN sits on his cot.)*

MOLINA. I don't understand. I'm leaving with more than I came
in with.
VALENTIN. *(Nodding to the AURORA poster.)* You're forget-
ting your friend.
MOLINA. I'm leaving her for you. She has great style and flare,
but I honestly think I have better legs. Here, I want you to have this.

(MOLINA hands VALENTIN a red shawl.)

VALENTIN. I don't think it's quite my style.
MOLINA. It's so you won't forget me, silly.
VALENTIN. There's no danger of that. *(Crossing to MOLINA.)*
Listen, Molina, there's something I want you to do.
MOLINA. Oh. Return the favor. Why did my blood just run cold?
VALENTIN. I want you to give someone a message for me.
MOLINA. No.

VALENTIN. It's very important.

MOLINA. I can't.

VALENTIN. I wouldn't ask you to do anything dangerous.

MOLINA. I'd go to places. I'm not brave like you.

VALENTIN. Yes, you are. I've seen you.

MOLINA. I don't want to get involved. I'm not like you. Don't try to change me. Leave me alone, Valentin, or I will betray you.

VALENTIN. I understand.

MOLINA. No, you don't. You couldn't. I'm sorry I can't be the man you want me to be. Stay well. Maybe I'll write. I'll never forget you.

VALENTIN. Molina, I want you to promise me something. I want you to promise me you'll never let anyone humiliate you ever again.

(VALENTIN takes MOLINA'S face in his hands and kisses him on the mouth.)

MOLINA. Give me your message.

VALENTIN. You'll deliver it?

(MOLINA quickly nods. VALENTIN pulls him close, whispers in his ear. We cannot hear his words.)

MOLINA. Yes... yes... I know where that is... I can remember a number... yes... is that all?

(ESTEBAN and MARCOS appear in the corridor outside the cell.)

ESTEBAN. Your chariot awaits you, your highness.

MOLINA. I've loved only two people in my life, before you. *(MOLINA embraces VALENTIN warmly and puts the red shawl around VALENTIN'S shoulders.)* Red's your color.

VALENTIN. It always was. *(MOLINA exits with ESTEBAN and MARCOS. VALENTIN speaks almost angrily.)* Come on, Molina. I'm counting on you. Be a man. Be a man!

(BLACKOUT)

Scene 6

(Music cue # 24 "OVER THE WALL 4")
(We follow MOLINA as he walks past the OTHER PRISONERS' cells, carrying his suitcases. He is on the way to the WARDEN'S office. ESTEBAN and MARCOS are following him. As he walks, we hear the prisoners sing.)

PRISONERS:
LUCKY MOLINA, SEE HOW HE GOES
OUT THERE OVER THE WALL

WHERE HE'LL BE GOING EVERYONE KNOWS
OUT THERE OVER THE WALL
OVER THE WALL

(MOLINA, ESTEBAN and MARCOS arrive at the WARDEN'S office. The WARDEN is waiting. They enter.)

WARDEN. Well, Molina, any names for me before you go?
MOLINA. Yes.

(Unable to speak out, MOLINA scribbles on a piece of paper from the WARDEN'S desk some names and hands them to the WARDEN.)

WARDEN. Well done. I knew I could count on you.
MOLINA. I'd like to go to my mother now.
WARDEN. Stay out of trouble this time. *(MOLINA turns to leave.)*
Molina! I'm glad I trusted you.

(MOLINA goes.)

MARCOS. You have the names?
WARDEN. *(Shaking his head.)* He made them up. The one I want he's taking with him. Follow him. Don't let him out of your sight. You don't sleep. You don't eat until he makes his move.
MARCOS. What if he's too frightened?
WARDEN. He's in love. He will make his move now.

(The WARDEN moves forward. The rest of the stage stays dark except for

silhouetted PRISONERS who sing contrapuntally to the following)
WARDEN:
I KNOW HIM
I KNOW HIM LIKE THE BACK
   OF MY HAND
                        PRISONERS:
                        LUCKY MOLINA
                        SEE HOW HE GOES

NEVER FEAR
I KNOW THAT QUEER
LIKE THE BACK OF MY HAND

                        WHERE HE'LL BE GOING
                        EVERYONE KNOWS

SO SETTLE BACK
JUST SIT STILL
HE'LL COME THROUGH
I KNOW HE WILL, I KNOW HIM
I KNOW HIM LIKE THE BACK
   OF MY HAND

                        OUT THERE OVER THE
                            WALL,
                        OVER THE WALL

HE'LL BE BACK IN THE LIFE
  HE KNOWS
THE MINUTE HE GOES...

                        THE MINUTE HE GOES

*(MOLINA runs into his apartment. He is still carrying his little suit-
case from the prison. He is so happy!)*

MOLINA. Mama! Mama! I'm home!
MOTHER. Luis, you've come, thank God! I'm so ashamed for
you to see me like this.
MOLINA. I'm going to take care of you now.
MOTHER. Don't ever leave me again. I couldn't bear it. Things
will be just like they were, you'll see.

WARDEN:
IN THE STORE WHERE THE ALLEY ENDS
HE'LL BE BACK WITH HIS FAIRY FRIENDS

WARDEN (cont.):
PUTTING PINS INTO LADIES CLOTHES

> **PRISONERS:**
> OUT THERE OVER THE WALL
> OVER THE WALL

(AURELIO, a WINDOW DRESSER appears wheeling a mannequin, He is busily dressing it up and chatting a mile a minute. MOLINA doesn't help with the work and seems numbed as AURELIO rattles on.)

AURELIO. You're lucky they kept your job open, darling. The queen who took over for you was a real bitch. There's a new salesman on the fifth floor who will make your heart beat. Tomasso! Is that a real man's name or is that a real man's name? What's the matter with you? You don't speak. You're not working. Where's my best friend?
MOLINA. I can't do this anymore, Aurelio.
AURELIO. What? Make our ladies beautiful?
MOLINA. Any of this.

(MOLINA walks away from AURELIO and the mannequin.)

AURELIO. Don't get uppity with me, Rio Rita. Remember, darling, I knew you when! What did they do to you in that prison?

(MUSIC up.)

> **PRISONERS:**
> OUT THERE OVER THE WALL
> OVER THE WALL

WARDEN:
AND THE WAITER HE ALWAYS
       WHINES ABOUT
HE'LL FERRET HIM OUT...

> **PRISONERS:**
> HE'LL FERRET HIM OUT...

(Lights up. MOLINA is waiting anxiously in a park. GABRIEL hurries in. He is in his waiter's apron.)

GABRIEL. I can't stay long. It's our busiest time.

MOLINA. We couldn't talk at the cafe. You look well. How are you? How is the family?

GABRIEL. Fine.

MOLINA. Did you get my letters?

GABRIEL. Yes.

MOLINA. I hope they weren't too—. *De trop*, as the French would say. Too much.

GABRIEL. I stopped reading them. I'm not your idea of me. I'm an ordinary man. I don't understand these things.

MOLINA. Yes, you do, Gabriel.

GABRIEL. Please don't come here again.

MOLINA. Why didn't you write me?

GABRIEL. I've got to go.

(GABRIEL hurries off. MUSIC up.)

                    PRISONERS:
                    OUT THERE OVER THE WALL,
                    OVER THE WALL

WARDEN:
HE'LL BE LEAVING HIS MAMA ALL ALONE
AND RUN FOR A PHONE...

                    PRISONERS:
                    HE'LL RUN FOR A PHONE...

(MOLINA returns to his MOTHER'S apartment.)

MOTHER. If you're caught, they'll send you back to jail.

MOLINA. It's only a call from a phone booth across the street. You can even watch me! There's no risk.

MOTHER. Then why are you giving me your savings?

MOLINA. Just in case. You know me. I'll be right back.

MOTHER. Must you do this, Luis?

MOLINA. I promised him.

MOTHER. You're all I have.

MOLINA. I won't do it [this] unless I have your blessing.

MOTHER. *(After a beat.)* Do what you must.

(MOTHER opens her arms to him. MOLINA embraces her and kisses her.)

MOLINA. I love you so much!

MOTHER. Now, go. Before I die another kind of death.

(The scene fades. We hear the sound of a phone ringing. Lights up on MARTA, who comes to answer it. She picks up the phone and we hear MOLINA'S voice on the other end.)

MARTA. Hello?

MOLINA. Marta?

MARTA. Yes?

MOLINA. I have a message from The Eagle. Christ has risen.

MARTA. I don't know what you're talking about. Who is this?

MOLINA. A friend. I can't talk. I'm being followed. They're right across the street. He's alive. He's well. He loves you.

MARTA. I don't want to get involved.

MOLINA. Neither did I.

MARTA. Who is this? Who are you? (The sound of the phone hanging up.) Hello? Hello?

(But MOLINA has hung up. We light up on PRISONERS.)

PRISONERS:
LUCKY MOLINA
BREATHING THE FREE, FRESH AIR
OVER THE WALL
LUCKY MOLINA
WISH IT WERE ME
OUT THERE
OVER THE WALL
OVER THE WALL
OVER THE WALL

PRISONERS (cont.):
OVER THE WALL!

(BLACKOUT)

Scene 7

The Interrogation Room

*(ESTEBAN and MARCOS are bringing VALENTIN on and will pre-
pare him for torture.)*

ESTEBAN. You though we'd forgotten you, 16115!
MARCOS. The warden has some new toys he wants to play with.
ESTEBAN. This whole prison of miserable scum and he want to
play with you.

(The WARDEN appears.)

WARDEN. I'm hoping we can settle this like reasonable men.
(VALENTIN spits at him.) Before you say "no" again, before you
parade your magnificent defiance, and God how I loathe that in a
man; it makes me want to destroy him all the more! *(HE grinds his
cigarette out on VALENTIN'S chest. ESTEBAN and MARCOS exit.)*
I want you to ask yourself: are your comrades really worth dying
for? Is you cause really going to change anything? Think it over, my
friend. In the meantime, you have a visitor. *(MARCOS and ESTEBAN
enter dragging a horribly bloodies PRISONER, whom they throw at
VALENTIN'S feet.)* Recognize your old friend, Valentin?

*(The GUARDS raise the PRISONER'S head. It is MOLINA.
VALENTIN cries out in recognition.)*

VALENTIN. No!!

WARDEN. We caught him in a phone booth making a call for your. But he won't tell us to whom, or give us the number. You made him brave, Valentin. Now make him less defiant. Tell him to talk, Valentin, talk or I'll blow his head off. Let him go.

MOLINA. Mission accomplished, captain. Awaiting further orders.

(MOLINA gives VALENTIN a crooked salute.)

WARDEN. Tell him to talk Valentin. I want names or he dies.

VALENTIN. What have I done?

MOLINA. Nothing, nothing, my Valentin.

VALENTIN. I betrayed you. Talk, give them what they want!

MOLINA. Darling, it all went right out of my dizzy head!

WARDEN. Last chance, Valentin.

VALENTIN. All right, I'll talk.

MOLINA. Then you *will* have betrayed me. *(The WARDEN takes out a pistol and puts it against MOLINA'S temple.)* I'm scared, Valentin. Look at me. Don't take your eyes off me!

WARDEN. I want names or he dies.

MOLINA. *(To VALENTIN.)* Write my mother if they'll let you.

WARDEN. *(To MOLINA.)* I'll give you three. One.

VALENTIN. Why are you doing this?

MOLINA. I want to. And Gabriel. Write him.

WARDEN. Two.

VALENTIN. Not for me. It isn't worth it.

MOLINA. Wouldn't it be funny if that were true?

WARDEN. Three. Who were you calling? Talk you fucking faggot or I'll blow your fucking head off.

(Music cue # 25 "ONLY IN THE MOVIES")

MOLINA. I love you...

(MUSIC. The WARDEN pulls the trigger. Pistol shot. MOLINA'S body slumps lifelessly. VALENTIN cries out convulsively.)

VALENTIN. Molina! Molina!

(WARDEN, ESTEBAN and MARCOS drag VALENTIN offstage.)

(MUSIC begins as MOLINA slowly rises. Suddenly, we see MOLINA'S
MOTHER carrying a flashlight. Behind her are three or four rows
of a movie theatre. VALENTIN takes a seat in the theatre. The
PRISONERS help MOLINA dress into white tie and tails. The
MOTHER, with her flashlight, leads the SPIDER WOMAN to a
seat. In the theatre we come to recognize our ENTIRE COMPANY:
GABRIEL, AURELIO, PRISONERS, the WARDEN, etc.
At the sight of MOLINA fully dressed in front of the AUDIENCE,
VALENTIN begins to applaud. The rest of the THEATRE AUDI-
ENCE joins him. MOLINA is receiving an ovation which he obvi-
ously savors. He turns and sings.)

MOLINA: **CHORUS:**
OPTIMISTIC ENDINGS
PASSIONATE ROMANCES
BEAUTIFULLY BEEFY HEROES
TAKING DEATH DEFYING CHANCES
ONLY IN THE MOVIES

DECOROUS MADONNAS
TOTALLY COMPLIANT
CHALLENGING THE VILLAIN BRAVELY
BOTH HIGH BUSTED AND DEFIANT
ONLY IN THE MOVIES   AH!

BUT MARBLE FLOORS TO GLIDE ON
AND LOOP THE LOOPS TO RIDE ON
AND SULTRY GIRLS BEGINNING SOME BEGUINE
I FOUND, AS I GREW OLDER
AND LIFE BECAME MUCH COLDER
WERE, TO MY SORROW,
NOWHERE TO BE SEEN

AND SO, I SPRAYED A LITTLE PERFUME   SPRAYED A
DABBED A LITTLE POWDER   LITTLE PERFUME
AND SUDDENLY THE MUTED STRINGS   DABBED A
                                        LITTLE POWDER

MOLINA (cont.):
BEGAN TO PLAY A LITTLE LOUDER
AND THOUGH I KNEW THE DIFFERENCE
I KEPT ON PRETENDING
I WAS IN THE MOVIES

BUT EVERYTHING CHANGED WHEN I MET YOU
YOU'VE CHANGED MY LIFE SOMEHOW

(VALENTIN rises from his theatre seat and joins MOLINA.)

EVERYTHING CHANGED WHEN I MET YOU
I FIND I WALK IN TECHNICOLOR NOW!

(The WARDEN'S voice rings out.)

WARDEN. *(Over a speaker.)* Talk you fucking faggot or I'll blow
your fucking head off!
OTHERS. Sssshh!

*(They pull the WARDEN back into his seat. Pistol Shot. MOLINA'S
head jerks back. He "dies" again. VALENTIN lifts MOLINA'S head,
cradling it in his arms.)*

MOLINA:
AND AS THIS PRINCESS LAY DYING
SHE RAISED HER LOVELY HEAD
AND AS HER LIVER KNELT BESIDE HER

THIS IS WHAT SHE SAID
LOOKING INTO THOSE STEELY BLUE EYES OF HIS
          SHE CRIED
'VIVA LA GUERRA'
'VIVA LA REVOLUCION'
'VIVA WHATEVER IT IS'

*(VALENTIN laughs, and as he does, we hear the SPIDER WOMAN'S
music. She rises from her theatre seat and goes to MOLINA. They*

tango as the COMPANY circles around them. VALENTIN faces
front. He sings.)

VALENTIN:
HIS NAME WAS MOLINA.

(Now the entire THEATRE AUDIENCE joins in and we hear this
strain over and over.)

ALL:
HIS NAME
WAS MOLINA
HIS NAME
WAS MOLINA
HIS NAME
WAS MOLINA

(MOLINA and SPIDER WOMAN kiss. The COMPANY cheers. Iris
Down.)

(BLACKOUT)

CURTAIN

END OF PLAY

FAVORITE MUSICALS *from* "The House of Plays"

PHANTOM

(All Groups) Book by Arthur Kopit. Music & Lyrics by Maury Yeston. Large cast of m. & f. roles—doubling possible. Various Ints. & Exts. This sensational new version of Gaston Leroux' *The Phantom of the Opera* by the team which gave you *Nine* wowed audiences and critics alike with its beautiful music and lyrics, and expertly crafted book, which gives us more background information on beautiful Christine Daee and the mysterious Erik than even the original novel does. Christine is here an untrained street singer discovered by Count Philippe de Chandon, champagne tycoon. Erik, the Phantom of the Opera, is the illegitimate son of a dancer and the opera's manager. He becomes obsessed with the lovely Christine because her voice reminds him of his dead mother's. "Reminiscent of *The Hunchback of Notre Dame, Cyrano de Bergerac* and *The Elephant Man, Phantom*'s love story—and the passionately soaring music it prompts—are deliciously sentimental. Add Erik's father lovingly acknowledging his parenthood as his son is dying and the show jerks enough tears to fill that Paris Opera Lagoon."—San Diego Union. "Yeston and Kopit get us to care about the characters by telling us a lot about them, some of it funny, but most of it poignant."—Houston Chronicle. **(#18958)**

Other Publications for Your Interest

MAIL
(ADVANCED GROUPS—MUSICAL)
Book & Lyrics by JERRY COLKER
Music by MICHAEL RUPERS
9 men, 6 women—2 Sets

What a terrific idea for a "concept musical"! As *Mail* opens Alex, an unpublished novelist, is having an acute anxiety attack over his lack of success in writing and his indecision regarding his girlfriend, Dana; so, he "hits the ground running" and doesn't come back for 4 months! When Alex finally returns to his apartment, he finds an unending stream of messages on his answering machine and stacks and stacks of unopened mail. As he opens his mail, it in effect comes to life, as we learn what has been happening with Alex's friends, and with Dana, during his absence. There is also some hilarious junk mail, which bombards Alex musically, as well as unpaid bills from the likes of the electric company (the ensemble comes dancing out of Alex's refrigerator singing "We're Gonna Turn Off Your Juice"). In the second act, we move into a sort of abstract vision of Alex's world, a blank piece of paper upon which he can, if he is able, and if he wishes, start over—with his writing, with his friends, with his father and, maybe, with Dana. Producers looking for something wild and crazy will, we know, want to open *this* MAIL, a hit with audiences and critics coast-to-coast, from the authors of THREE GUYS NAKED FROM THE WAIST DOWN! "At least 12 songs are solid enough to stand on their own. If MAIL can't deliver, there is little hope for the future of the musical theatre, unless we continue to rely on the British to take possession of a truly American art form."—Drama-Logue. "Make room for the theatre's newest musical geniuses."—The Same. (Terms quoted on application. Music available on rental. See p. 48.)

(#15199)

CHESS
(ADVANCED GROUPS—MUSICAL/OPERA)
Book by RICHARD NELSON
Lyrics by TIM RICE
Music by BJORN ULVAEUS & BENNY ANDERSSON
9 men, 2 women, 1 female child, plus ensemble

A *musical* about an *international chess match?!?!* A bad idea from the get-go, you'd think; but no—Tim Rice (he of *Evita, Joseph and the Amazing Technicolor Dreamcoat* and *Jesus Christ Superstar*), Bjorn Ulvaeus and Benny Andersson (they of Swedish Supergroup ABBA) and noted American playwright Richard Nelson, all in collaboration with Trevor Nunn (*Les Miz., Nick Nick*, etc.) have pulled it off, creating an extraordinary rock opera about international intrigue which uses as a metaphor a media-drenched chess match between a loutish American champion (shades of Bobby Fischer) and a nice-guy Soviet champion. The American has a girlfriend, Florence, there in Bangkok (where the match takes place) to be his second and to provide moral support. There she meets, and falls in love with, Anatoly, the Soviet champion—and the sparks fly, particularly when Anatoly decides to defect to the west, causing a postponement and change of venue to Budapest. Eventually, it is clear that all the characters are merely pawns in a larger chess match between the C.I.A. and the KGB! The pivotal role of Florence is perhaps the most extraordinary and complex role in the musical theatre since Eva Peron; and the roles of Freddie and Anatoly (both tenors) are great, too. Several of the songs have become international hits, including Florence's "Heaven Help My Heart", "I know Him So Well" and "Nobody's On Nobody's Side", and Freddie's descent into the maelstrom of decadence, "One Night in Bangkok". Playing to full houses and standing ovations, *Chess* closed exceedingly prematurely on Broadway; and, perhaps the story behind *that* just might make the basis of another Rice/ABBA/Nelson/Nunn collaboration! (Terms quoted on application. Music available on rental. See p. 48.) Slightly restricted.

(#5236)

Other Publications for Your Interest

ANGRY HOUSEWIVES
(LITTLE THEATRE—MUSICAL)
Book & Lyrics by A.M. COLLINS
Music & Lyrics by CHAD HENRY

4 men, 4 women—Various sets.

Bored with their everyday, workaday lives and kept in insignificance by their boyfriends/ husbands—these really are four *angry* housewives. They try a number of things in search of personal fulfillment, but nothing strikes a chord until one of them strikes a chord on her guitar, and gets the idea that, well, why don't they form a punk-rock group and enter the upcoming talent show down at the neighborhood punk club? Of course they form the group, of course they enter, and of course they win, calling themselves—of course—"The Angry Housewives", winning the contest—and stopping the show—with their punk-rock song. This genial satire of contemporary feminism ran for ages in Seattle, and has had numerous successful productions cross-country. "The show is insistently outrageous, frequently funny, occasionally witty and altogether irresistible."—Seattle Times. Slightly Restricted. **Posters.**

(#3931)

NUNSENSE
(LITTLE THEATRE—MUSICAL)
By DAN GOGGIN

5 women—Unit sets.

This delightful Off Broadway hit will certainly tickle your audience's funnybone. It's about the efforts of the Order of the Little Sisters of Hoboken (a nunnery, of course) to raise money to bury the remaining four of the fifty-two nuns who have died of botulism contracted by eating vichysoise prepared by the convent chef, Sister Julia (Child of God). Our five nuns have somehow been spared the fate of the other sisters, as they were playing bingo that night at another parish. *Nunsense*, then, is the fund-raising show they are presenting to us in hopes we will help them with the necessary cash. ". . . a lively 'nunstop' musical."—N.Y. Times. One of the feistiest shows around."—WNEW-TV. "Clever and amusing."—Catholic Transcript. "Good-natured. A cheerful evening."—Catholic Standard. Winner, 1986 Outer Critics Circle Award. Best Off-Broadway Musical. Slightly Restricted.

(#16074)